Rise of the Dominants

The Russian Reborn: Rise of the Dominants
Final Book of the Trilogy

Cover by Shanoff Designs
Formatted by BB eBooks
Phoenix symbol by Nicole Delfs

Dedication

This is dedicated to a sweet friend and fan, Ceej Chargualaf, who died much too young. A blogger and book lover, she and I became fast friends when she offered to create a bible for the Brie's Submission series. Ceej fell in love with the characters and we had countless conversations about them. She was so enthusiastic about each new book coming out that she would make cool graphics to share with other readers.

But it wasn't her love of my books or her awesome review skills that I adored, it was her warrior spirit and her love for life. Even though she fought pain every day, she made it a point to share her light and love with the world. I felt truly honored to call her my friend.

Ceej, I dedicate Rytsar's book to you. Thank you for all the love you poured out to me and my characters. You truly made a difference in my life and will live on forever in this story.

Love, Red

SIGN UP FOR MY NEWSLETTER HERE FOR THE LATEST RED PHOENIX UPDATES

SALES, GIVEAWAYS, NEW RELEASES, PREORDER LINKS, AND MORE!

SIGN UP HERE

REDPHOENIXAUTHOR.COM/NEWSLETTER-SIGNUP

Don't miss the first two books in the trilogy!

Sir's Rise:

Rise of the Dominants Book One
Available Now

Master's Fate:

Rise of the Dominants Book Two
Available Now

CONTENTS

Kinky Celebrations

Hell, yes!

I've just aced my last final, completing my sophomore year of college, and now I crave some serious celebration. This last semester kicked my ass with all the damn projects and papers I had to wade through.

While I've had no problem understanding the material, I can't stomach all the busy work my professors have subjected me to this year. It's no surprise to me when I'm the first student to walk out of class after successfully completing my last final.

Heading off to my best friend's dorm building, I get on the phone. I want to make certain everything is set for the afternoon I have planned before I knock on his door. When Thane doesn't answer, I knock even harder.

I know he's in there but, for some strange reason, the guy has been acting like a recluse for the past week. "Open up, comrade. I need to speak with you."

I smile in satisfaction when the doorknob slowly turns. As soon as the door swings open, I grab Thane's shirt, pulling him out into the hallway.

"What the hell?" he growls in protest, trying to break away from my tight grip.

"Enough of this hiding. We're heading out."

"The fuck I am," he states, attempting to drag me back into his room. He struggles but can't break my grasp because this Russian isn't budging.

"Your best friend just completed a semester from hell. It is your duty to entertain me," I tell him.

Thane shakes his head, his voice becoming serious. "I suggest you find someone else. I'd only bring you down today."

"I won't take no for an answer."

I start dragging him toward the elevator. When he tries to fight against me, I remind him, "Remember the night I invited you to the dungeon for the first time? You reacted this way and we both know how that turned out."

Thane stops resisting and actually cracks a smile. "Fine. Just let me lock the damn door and get my tools for the dungeon."

"The dungeon isn't open for another six hours," I inform him, amused he's forgotten that.

Thane laughs at himself. "Hell, I've lost all track of time."

"What's going on with you?"

He shakes his head. "If it's my duty to entertain you today, we'll talk about that later."

I want to press him on the issue, but I am too wound up. "Fine. We'll discuss it tomorrow—because, right now, it's time to party!"

Thane smiles, but I know it's forced because it doesn't reach his eyes.

Luckily, I can remedy that, and smack him hard on the back. "You won't need your tools where we're going, comrade. I have arranged something extraordinary for us."

I drive him to our destination without informing him where we're headed. As we pull up, he gives me a confused look. "Wait. Isn't this glee's place?"

"It is," I answer with a smirk.

"Is she back?" he asks hopefully.

"*Nyet*, comrade. Glee is never coming back."

I note the disappointment on his face, but I understand. Glee was a special girl and that fivesome we had together before we sent her off to explore the world is something I will never forget.

But life marches on.

I give him a mischievous smile, knowing the fun ahead for us. "Trust me. You won't miss glee today."

Giving him no further explanation, I head toward the house. I'm encouraged when he follows behind me.

Ringing the doorbell, we're greeted with nervous giggles on the other side of the door.

I glance sideways at Thane. "They sound anxious. That pleases me."

He chuckles. "Of course it would, you sadist."

The door opens and four scantily clad girls stand before us, their faces covered with veils of various colors.

They lower their eyes in respect.

"Thank you for coming, Rytsar," the four say in unison.

"I haven't come yet," I correct them.

Glee's former roommates twitter in response. Thane and I have scened individually with all four submissives at the dungeon, but this will be the first time we've played together as a group.

The fact that this is taking place in their home, instead of the dungeon, makes this interaction even more intimate.

The girls turn their attention to Thane, speaking as one. "Sir Davis, we are honored you've agreed to join us today."

Thane glances at me, unsure of what I have planned. It's understandable he feels nervous, seeing how I'm a sadist. However, today is all about indulgence. I deserve it after the months of hell I've been through—and so does my friend.

Surprised they haven't invited me in yet, I glance around and shrug.

Shade bows, while the other three subs, luna, vixen and indigo, look embarrassed by the oversight. "Rytsar, we welcome you into our home."

The girls part so that we can enter, and then all four kneel on the floor and bow to us as if we are kings.

"Your will is our pleasure," luna states reverently, looking up at me, her sapphire eyes enhanced by the copper veil she wears.

"Show me the room you've prepared," I command.

Luna stands gracefully, gesturing to the back room. "We have everything ready for you, Rytsar," she states with a subtle undertone of pride which is characteristic of a devoted submissive.

I nod to Thane before heading down the hallway behind her.

I whistle in appreciation when I walk into the room. The girls have outdone themselves, transforming the large bedroom into an oasis of pleasure. Gossamer fabric cascades from the center of the ceiling to all four walls, and the floor is covered in colorful pillows of every shape and size.

Instead of a bed, a low-set table is set in the center of the room with all my favorite tools lined up in neat rows, including my cat o' nines.

When Thane joins me, along with the other girls, I ask him, "Aren't you glad I invited you, comrade?" Leaning in, I whisper, "It's so much better than brooding in your dorm room."

He bumps his shoulder against mine and cracks a smile.

I knew I could bring him out of his funk!

Looking back at the girls, my cock swells with desire. There is nothing more captivating than the submission of four women at the same time. The fact that Thane is here with me makes it that much more entertaining.

Since he is here as my guest, I ask, "What would you like to begin with first?"

He looks down at the four kneeling girls and chuckles lightly. "The possibilities are endless."

"*Da*, they are, comrade," I agree, placing my hand on his shoulder. "Tell me something you have yet to experience."

He thinks about it for a moment before surprising me with his answer. "I haven't done an anal scene."

The girls gasp softly but keep their eyes focused on the floor.

I walk Thane out of the room, looking at him suspiciously. "The entire time you've been at the dungeon you haven't fucked a girl in the ass?"

He shrugs, looking nonplussed.

"Is there a reason?" I demand. I am suspicious of any man who doesn't partake in anal sex.

"No. I've simply been interested in exploring other things."

I shake my head in disbelief. "And because of that error in judgment, you've missed out on some of the most stimulating sex a man can experience."

Thane huffs. "I sincerely doubt that."

Raising an eyebrow, I ask him, "How can you know if you haven't tried it?"

He snorts, conceding, "True enough."

I slap him on the back before heading into the room.

"Who would like to be Sir Davis's first?"

Shade immediately raises her hand before the other three have a chance to respond. Because she helped me before with a scene where I introduced Thane to my cat o' nines, shade seems the perfect choice.

Looking at the three other submissive, I command huskily, "You will pleasure my cock while I watch my comrade claim shade's sexy ass for the first time."

I can feel the synergy in the room increase—all of us invested in sharing this first-time experience with Thane.

There is something alluring about watching a person's initial introduction to anal sex, be it male or female.

I lie down on a mound of pillows and make myself

comfortable before gesturing to my subs to join me.

Luna whispers something to vixen, and I distinctly hear my name mentioned.

"What did you just say?" I ask her.

She turns to face me, momentarily mute, as her eyes grow wide.

I raise an eyebrow and wait for her to respond.

"I…umm…told vixen, 'I can't believe I'm about to scene with Rytsar Superstar.'"

I hear Thane snicker under his breath, but I manage to keep a straight face.

"Rytsar Superstar…" I repeat in a serious tone, although I have to admit I like the way it rolls off my tongue.

She nods slowly, unsure of my reaction and fearful of my punishment.

I glance at Thane, giving him a superior look before responding to her. "I will allow the name, but never when you speak to me directly."

"Of course not, Rytsar!" she replies, bowing her head humbly before settling in between my legs. At the same time, vixen and indigo sit gracefully on either side of me.

I wrap my arms around the two closest ones, smiling lustfully with the knowledge my cock will be well pleased today.

Looking back at Thane, the four of us wait.

Thane now understands that he is the center of attention. Rather than shy away from his role, I'm proud to see him embrace it.

Looking down at the table, he picks up the tube of lubricant and slips it into his pocket.

He then turns to shade and orders, "Take off the veil. I want to see that beautiful face again."

Shade gracefully detaches the thin veil and lets it flutter to the floor.

"That's what I wanted to see," Thane growls huskily, fisting her hair as he moves in for a kiss.

My cock stirs as I watch him advance on her, but I let my shaft continue to ache while I casually observe them. I enjoy the sexual torment of it, knowing my subs eagerly wait for my command to descend upon it.

As Thane deepens his kisses, his hands begin roving over shade's curvaceous body, removing any fabric that gets in his way.

Soon she is completely naked before us.

Thane's hand disappears between her legs and she begins to moan as he teases her clit. I can feel the increasing sexual tension build in my three subs while they watch Thane's scene unfold before them.

I savor the sensual torture the four of us are experiencing as we lie there watching the two, but I have to reprimand luna when she moves her veil aside to taste my precome with her tongue.

She instantly blushes. "Forgive me, Rytsar."

It pleases me that she finds my cock so hard to resist. Being in a generous mood, I accept her apology without punishment, commanding her to turn her attention back on Thane.

I glance up at my friend, watching as his hands slowly moves up to shade's large tits, pinching her nipples between his wet fingers.

Shade moans in pleasure, her hips instinctively gyrating against him.

Grasping one of her breasts, he brings it to his mouth, sucking off the remnants of her juices. Upon tasting her, he lets out a low animal growl that sends an electric current of desire through the room.

We all know he wants to claim her.

Letting go of shade, Thane suddenly sweeps all the neatly placed tools off the table, ordering her to get on all fours.

Shade climbs onto the table, facing us with a look of excitement as he caresses her ass with both hands.

I have to hand it to Thane. He knows how to make a dramatic scene.

Taking the lube from his pocket, he stares at it for a moment.

I know my friend. He normally researches everything he does before playing it out with a sub, and I've sprung this on Thane with no chance for him to plan for the scene.

Highly experienced in this area, I decide to take charge so he can thoroughly enjoy this gift I've given him.

"Cover your finger with the lubricant, comrade, and let me watch you explore her tight ass. Acclimate her body to your touch while you coat her on the inside."

Thane nods in acknowledgment, covering his finger with the lubricant. Positioning himself behind her, he affirms his dominance by spanking her right ass cheek, causing her to squeak and then giggle excitedly while I watch the skin on her ass pinken.

He makes eye contact with me once, before turning

all his attention on shade.

"Does it excite you to know I've never done this before?" he asks her.

"Yes, Sir…it does," she purrs loudly.

He runs his finger over the valley between her ass cheeks, rimming the outside of her pink rosette with lubricant, continuing to tantalize her with his touch.

Shade arches her back, inviting him to explore more of her, as she stares directly into my eyes.

I am fucking turned on at this point knowing what's about to happen, and tell luna to remove her veil. I then push her head down so she can finally taste my cock. When luna moans on my shaft, I'm forced to close my eyes before I lose control.

Her mouth is warm and her tongue is far too talented…

"Please, Sir," shade begs Thane.

I open my eyes and order luna to stop. Wanting her to observe them, I turn her head so she can watch as Thane lets out a low groan as he slips his finger into shade. Taking his time to explore her, he prepares her for his manly invasion.

Shade bites her bottom lip, pressing herself against his hand, begging for more of him.

"Are you ready for two fingers?" Thane asks huskily.

"Please, Sir," she purrs.

Thane recoats his fingers with lubricant and pushes both fingers inside her. I can tell by the concentrated look on his face that he is not only coating the inside of her, but also finding those sensitive areas she responds to.

As he pushes his fingers in deeper, he murmurs, "That's it, shade. Vocalize your pleasure for your Master."

Responding to the sounds of her passionate moans, I command my other two subs to lose their veils so all three can pleasure my cock. I groan in satisfaction as luna sucks my balls, while vixen and indigo take turns teasing my cock with their tongues.

All the tension from the past semester completely vanishes as I give into the sensation of three mouths licking, tasting, nipping, and sucking my hard shaft.

Holy fuck, it's good to be me.

I stop them when I see Thane starting to undress. I can tell he is desperate to claim shade but in his eagerness to take her, I don't want him to miss out on the full sensation of his first entry.

"Go slowly as you penetrate her," I instruct. "Make shade aware of every inch of you."

While Thane finishes undressing, I reposition my subs, commanding vixen and indigo to get on all fours and face shade so they can continue to watch her. I then order luna to change positions so she can lay her head on my stomach and tease my cock with her tongue as she watches the scene play out.

Once all of my girls are ready, I put my hands between vixen and indigo's legs and slip my fingers into their pussies at the same time, groaning at the decadence of it.

I hear the slippery sound of Thane applying the lubricant to his shaft and look up as he positions himself behind shade, placing his hands on her firm buttocks.

"Look Rytsar in the eye as I slide my cock into you."

She whimpers in excitement, lifting her ass to him.

Thane has the look of raw desire as he grasps his rock-hard shaft and presses it against her resistant hole. "Take all of me." His command is a low, husky growl as he slowly pushes the head of his cock into her tight ass.

I watch the expression on both their faces the moment his shaft breaches her opening. She has a look of carnal satisfaction as his thick cock begins to fill her. At the same time, Thane's eyes are closed as he concentrates on every centimeter of her tight embrace as he claims her.

I remember my first time with anal. The ecstasy of having your cock squeezed tightly as you push in and pull out is like nothing else.

Thane is experiencing that now and, by the sounds of his low groans, he's enjoying it too much and is struggling to control his climax while he experiences all the overwhelming sensations. I'm not surprised when he pulls out to give himself a few seconds to recover. He slaps her ass again as he pushes his cock back into her.

I groan and feel the rush of wetness around my fingers as both vixen and indigo respond to the scene. That's when luna kicks it up a notch, wrapping her warm lips around my cock.

I hold my breath as I take in the multiple sensations—the erotic feel of their wet pussies, the warmth and suction of luna's mouth, and the kinky vision of Thane fucking shade in the ass.

Thane changes the angle of his strokes and begins to thrust deeper. Shade responds with screams of pleasure just before she comes.

I almost climax just watching her.

Not wanting to orgasm alone, I command vixen and indigo to come as I stroke their swollen clits with my thumbs.

Indigo is the first to reach climax, followed a few seconds later by vixen. Feeling the rhythmic pulses of their orgasms, my balls tighten as the ache builds to unbearable levels. I push my cock deep into luna's throat and let out a roar of satisfaction as I come.

In this moment, I am fully male.

As I feed luna the last of my seed, I hear the telltale sounds of Thane's impending orgasm as he starts panting in low, grunting gasps. I smile to myself. From my vantage point, I can see the skin of shade's ass rippling from the impact of each hard thrust. Thane isn't holding back and, by the look of pure rapture on shade's face, it's exactly what she needs.

Both cry out with animalistic screams of passion when he grabs her hips and forcefully delivers his come deep in her ass.

Afterward, he pulls out slowly and gathers shade into his arms, speaking softly in her ear. She nods as he speaks, and I'm left wondering what it is he is saying to her.

Thane always seeks interactions with his subs after a scene. It is not something I've seen my father ever do and was not common in the circle of sadists I ran with in Russia, but I find it intriguing.

Instead of whispering in luna's ear, I pull her beside me and open her legs wide. She's just given me an expert blow job without coming herself, and I want to reward her efforts. Telling the other two to play with her tits, I bring luna to climax with my tongue.

Most men have no idea how to pleasure multiple women at once, but that has never been an issue for me. I am conscious of each one, and know what I need from them and what they need from me.

Even though eating her turns me on, feeling her intense orgasm against my mouth really stirs my libido, making my cock rigid again.

Wiping her wetness from my lips, I nod to Thane. "Comrade, get me my 'nines which you so rudely threw to the floor in your need to fuck."

He chuckles, giving shade a kiss on the forehead before getting up to retrieve my whip. In the process of finding it, he picks up several pairs of nipple clamps. "I'll entertain the others while you caress that one with your cat o' nines."

"I like the way you think…"

After hours of play, Thane and I leave the girls sore and satiated.

I notice on the drive back that he has a grin that won't go away.

"So you enjoyed anal, comrade?"

His smile grows. "That's an understatement."

"Don't you feel foolish for waiting so long?"

Thane chuckles. "It was certainly an oversight on my

part."

I nod. "I was worried for a moment. Had you passed up the opportunity, I would have had to call our friendship off."

He laughs. "Why?"

"A man afraid to experience the pleasure of a tight ass is no friend of mine."

He shakes his head, chuckling. "You're very strange, Durov."

"Strange, but right."

I'm glad to see Thane acting more like himself and comment, "A good session certainly helps to put things in perspective, doesn't it?"

He gives me a sideways glance. "How do you mean?"

"After a satisfying scene, everything else comes into focus. Do you not feel more relaxed and in control of your life?"

He smiles. "I do."

"That is the power of BDSM. It takes the physical and mixes it with the spiritual so there is internal balance."

Thane nods, looking out the window. "You may be right."

When I arrive at his dorm building, I park the car without getting out.

"You've got other plans?" he asks.

"*Da*. I have a date with vodka and my countrymen."

"Want me to join you?"

I laugh, knowing he would be the first to pass out, and I do not want my Russian friends shaving his eyebrows or leaving Thane naked in a public place. "Best you do not, comrade."

He shrugs. "Good, I don't care for hangovers any-way." Thane then slaps me on the back. "So, go forth and annihilate your fellow Russians."

I grin, stating with confidence, "They stand no chance against me."

Colliding Forces

After a successful night of partying with my fellow Russians, I stagger back to my dorm. Next thing I know, I'm waking up on the ground, outside my dorm building with Anderson and Samantha looking down at me.

"You all right there, buddy?"

I smile, feeling completely at home in my inebriated state.

"Looks like someone did a little too much celebrating," Anderson comments as he grabs my hand and helps me to my feet.

Samantha takes hold of my other arm for support.

She smells nice.

They help me into my building, and Anderson presses the button for the elevator. While we wait, I turn my head and smirk at Samantha. "Well, hello, beautiful."

"Hey, my drunken Russian."

I grin, riding the high of the alcohol in my bloodstream and my intense attraction to the girl.

When the doors open, Samantha states, "I can take it from here."

"Are you sure?" Anderson asks her.

"Absolutely."

With my arm wrapped tightly around Samantha, I stare at my friend Anderson, smirking at the guy as the elevator doors close between us.

As the elevator rises, I momentarily lose my balance, my head still swimming from the excessive amount of vodka I've consumed.

Samantha steadies me, laughing under her breath.

Feeling as if everything is in slow motion, I turn my head toward her and ask, "Did you have a good time with him tonight?"

"It was very vanilla, but still fun." She looks at me with an amused expression. "Why? Are you jealous?"

"*Nyet.*"

Her red lips curl into a captivating smile. "Are you sure?"

I snort, before grabbing the back of her neck and kissing her possessively.

When the elevator suddenly jolts to a stop at my floor, it unbalances me again and I stumble as I walk out into the hallway.

"How much have you had to drink?"

I grin, stating proudly, "I was the last man standing tonight."

She shakes her head, laughing. "Considering you were drinking with Russians, that says a lot."

"*Da.* No one outdrinks a Durov." I attempt to get my key to fit in the damn keyhole, but fail several times.

Samantha takes it from me and unlocks the door, guiding me inside. "Wow, you have quite the setup here. My dorm room looks paltry by comparison."

"Only the best for a Durov," I joke, as I stumble to my bed and lay down on it.

Looking up at her, I pat the area beside me.

She purses those kissable lips. "I really don't think I should stay."

"Why not?"

"It's after hours and I'm not allowed here."

"Everyone is out partying. Who is going to stop you?"

She smiles as she steps nearer to the bed. "You have a convincing argument."

"Of course, I do…"

When she sits down beside me, the fog of alcohol suddenly dissipates as if I haven't spent an entire evening drinking everyone under the table.

Her presence seems to have an unusual effect on me, and I now find myself in serious need of her pussy.

I lean against her, pushing her down on the bed, and begin ravaging her mouth with my tongue. Her long fingernails scratch my back through the material of my shirt as she responds to my raging need.

"Lose the shirt," she growls hungrily.

"Only if you lose yours," I counter.

The two of us can't be near each other without wanting to fuck, but we must always dance around the power exchange between us—each of us wanting to dominate the other.

She huffs in irritation, used to getting her own way

with men. "I can't believe I've fallen for a dominant male…" she mutters.

Samantha has submitted to me only a couple of times since we've become serious. Being a Dominant herself makes it a tricky business for both of us.

Whenever she requests taking on the submissive role, I must plan the scene out carefully.

It has proven a worthy challenge, and we both find it rewarding on those rare occasions when she dabbles with her submissive side. For Samantha, it's a chance to visit another aspect of herself, while I get to enjoy the thrill of mastering a fellow Dominant.

It's a win-win for both of us, but I have to take extreme care not to damage the powerful dynamic between us. It's important that I break down her need for control during our scene while still respecting her dominant nature. Not many men can handle such a difficult challenge, but I find it exhilarating.

Watching her come multiple times under my skillful and calculated guidance is a high I can't match.

Outside of those exchanges, however, we fight for control as we ravage each other's bodies. There have been times when she has drawn blood with her fingernails, and I have left bruises on her skin from multiple bite marks.

Tonight is no different.

We rip off our shirts and she loses her bra, before we go for each other, pressing naked skin against naked skin.

When I feel her nails raking my bare back, I immediately go for her throat, biting until she stops and relaxes in my embrace.

I pull away to admire the deep indents my teeth have made on her white skin, while I savor the sting of her scratches on my back.

I hunger for Samantha, needing to thrust my cock deep into her wet pussy, but she is playing hard to get—as she always does.

Biting my bottom lip, she pulls away intentionally causing pain. "Not so fast, big boy. This woman needs a drink." She looks around my dorm room curiously, asking, "Got anything besides vodka here?"

I tilt my head, wondering why she would want anything else. "Yes. In my cabinet. I have a stash for my friends who have no taste."

She laughs as she walks over to the cabinet and opens it wide. "Look at all the toys you have…"

I glance proudly at the fine selection of quality BDSM tools. "I like to be prepared for any occasion."

"Umm…" She looks them over with admiration. "But, where's the liquor?"

"Look for a tiny button on the upper right-hand corner."

When she finds it, it causes the back to slide down, revealing a stock of various liquors. She purrs in satisfaction before crying out, "You have Gran Platinum."

"I was told Patron is an excellent tequila."

"You haven't even tried it?"

"Why would I? It's not vodka."

She grabs the bottle and a couple of shot glasses. "You haven't lived until you've had Platinum. My dad used to let me take sips from his glass when my mom wasn't looking."

Samantha unceremoniously breaks the seal on the bottle and pours two shots.

I chuckle when she hands it to me.

"What?" she asks, crinkling her nose in a girlish manner.

"Nothing," I answer as my gaze drifting down to her beautiful tits.

Samantha nods to me before taking her shot, making a purr of delight after she swallows it.

I follow suit, noting the unique burn of the Mexican liquor.

"What do you think?" she asks, smiling.

"It's…different."

"That's all you have to say?" Samantha protests. "This is the smoothest tequila ever made and all you have to say is that it's *different*? You didn't give it enough of a chance." She pours another shot, thrusting the glass at me.

I down the second shot, still not enamored with the tequila. However, I'm amused by the intense way she's staring at me.

"Well?"

Not wanting to ruin a perfectly good evening with my honest answer, I say, "It's a smooth tequila."

"Right?" she cries enthusiastically, reaching out to pour me another.

But I hold onto my shot glass. "I've had enough."

When she frowns in disappointment, I remind her, "I did just drink my classmates under the table tonight, remember?"

"Fine." She pouts. "Then I'll drink alone, Mr. Durov."

I reach out and pull her onto my lap, bottle and all. "I like a woman who can handle her alcohol."

She raises an eyebrow. "You do, do you?" Tipping the bottle up with both hands, she drinks directly from it, letting the clear liquid dibble from her lips down to the valley between her breasts.

Wiping her luscious mouth afterward, she turns back to me. "You've never been around me when I drink tequila, have you?"

"*Nyet*. I have not." The daring look in her eyes amuses me.

Her pupils widen as she proclaims, "I can get a little crazy on the stuff."

It sounds intriguing, and I command huskily, "Lean forward and let me taste that tequila again." Smashing my face between her breasts, I lick the tangy liquor directly from her skin.

Samantha moans like a cat in heat, dragging her nails down my back.

I respond by kissing her more roughly, penetrating her mouth with my tongue. I'm so lost in the taste of her that I don't notice when my head starts spinning again as the tequila interacts with the vast amounts of vodka already in my bloodstream.

I pull back, momentarily disoriented, and attempt to shake off the dizziness.

Samantha takes the opportunity to grab my wrists, forcing them above my head as she presses my body down on the bed.

Staring at me, she purrs, "Damn, you do look good like this…"

The blood starts pounding in my ears as the room spins at an even faster pace just before I pass out.

I open my eyes when I feel someone patting my cheek.

"There we are, big boy…" Samantha murmurs seductively. "You can't go falling asleep on me like that."

I try to sit up and suddenly become aware that I am not only completely naked, but my wrists have also been tied to the headboard.

My heart starts pounding as I pull against the ropes that bind me. I glare at her. "*Nyet!*"

She runs a red fingernail down my chest, smiling. "Yes, Rytsar Durov. Tonight, you are finally going to submit to me."

I struggle against the ropes, but the alcohol coursing through my bloodstream makes my movements sluggish and ineffective.

"That's right, Rytsar…" she purrs. "I am going to introduce you to your submissive side."

I don't have a damn submissive side to me. Everything within my soul fights against the idea.

"Samantha, this is a hard limit. I *cannot* submit to you."

"You say that now…" She lets out a light laugh, picking up her glass and downing another shot of tequila.

I find it difficult to swallow, realizing she is not listening to me. "Samantha," I say in a sterner voice, "you do *not* have my consent. I refuse to submit."

"Oh, I'm not asking your permission, big boy," she answers, laughing with a seductive tone. "I demand your submission."

I shake my head, but then close my eyes when the room starts spinning again.

Completely ignoring my inebriated state, she informs me, "Although you have so many fun toys to play with, I've got one I just purchased that I want to try."

I feel the bed move as she leans in close, kissing me on the cheek. "Don't move," she teases as she stands up.

I open one eye and watch as she disappears out the door. Breathing a sigh of relief, I give into the spinning room and drift into oblivion.

I reawaken to the tight grasp of a hand on my cock. I groan in pleasure, thinking it's a dream.

"I thought that would wake you."

Opening my eyes, I'm surprised to find Samantha sitting on my bed, stroking my hard cock with both hands.

"What are you doing here?" I croak, too drunk to remember what's happened.

"You may address me as Mistress," she replies in a commanding tone.

Mistress?

A cold chill courses through my body as my memory

slowly returns. I look down to see my ankles are now bound.

"Untie me!"

She answers my command with a cool smile.

Needing Samantha to understand she's about to cross a serious line, I tell her, "I'm calling my safeword—Red. Do you hear me? R.E.D. I cannot be any clearer with you. Stop this now." Looking up at my bound wrists, I order, "Unbind me, Samantha."

She shakes her head with a devilish glint in her eye. "You claim you are incapable of submitting, but…" Tightening her grip on my cock, she leans forward and whispers, "You will, whether you want to or not."

Through gritted teeth, I warn her, "I will never forgive you if you go through with this."

She sits back, looking shocked. "But why?"

"I cannot submit. I do not say it as a challenge. It's a fact."

Samantha dismisses my statement with a huff. "Well, I'll see about that…"

She presses her red lips against the head of my cock, but her actions toward me have robbed me of any feelings of desire I had for her, and my shaft becomes limp in her hand.

"Release me," I order again, my anger growing.

"You're not the one in control here," she informs me, pursing her red lips. Picking up the ball gag from my stash of toys, she says, "From now on, you're not allowed to speak."

I glare hard at her as she approaches. "If you care anything for me, unbind me now and leave."

She pouts, sticking out her bottom lip. "How is it fair that I've submitted to you, yet you refuse to submit to me?"

"You did so willingly," I remind her, staring at the ball gag as she brings it closer to my mouth.

"I deserve your submission," she insists, sounding like a spoiled child.

"It's not in my nature."

"I don't believe you," she coos, giving me a flirtatious smile.

"Then you don't know me."

"Hah!" Samantha exclaims, pouring herself another shot. "I know all kinds of things about you, Rytsar Durov." Smiling, her gaze travels leisurely over my naked body. "You showed me the freedom of submission and I know, once you experience my dominance, you'll be begging to serve me."

"You're wrong." My muscles tighten across my abs as I struggle against my bonds.

"No, I'm not wrong," she says as she forces the ball gag into my mouth, buckling the strap behind my head.

Afterward, she looks down at me, smiling with satisfaction. Undoing her jeans, Samantha slips her hand underneath her panties and starts stroking her clit. "I could come just looking at you all bound and helpless."

After playing with herself for several minutes, she takes her wet fingers and tries to swipe them across my lips, but I turn my head in disgust.

Samantha laughs cruelly. "Oh, do you think you can disrespect your Mistress like that?"

I hear her rummaging through my cabinet again.

When she returns, I hear the distinctive sound of a cane cutting through the air.

I close my eyes when the first strike of the instrument explodes against my thigh. I'm determined to endure her abuse the same way I did as a boy at the whipping pole when my father beat me.

When Samantha sees I'm not responding to her punishment, she changes tactics and puts the cane down. Caressing my face with both hands, she slowly turns my head and forces me to look into her eyes. "I have a special present for you."

Leaning over, she picks up an instrument from my nightstand and holds it up for me to see. "Do you know what this is?"

Disinterested, I glance at the metal instrument she holds in her hand.

"This is meant to stimulate the penis." She looks down at my limp cock. "Which should help with the little problem you seem to be having."

I hate her for making light of this abusive situation and struggle against my bonds.

At this point, Samantha is oblivious to me, caught up in her own power trip. "My handsome Russian, you and I are going to connect in a way you've never experienced before," she says excitedly, her eyes sparkling with drunken excitement.

Bile rises in my throat as I watch her meticulously clean the instrument she plans to use on me.

"I bought only the finest surgical lubricant. I don't want anything happening to that handsome cock of yours," she informs me as she starts coating the thin, three-inch long section of the instrument with lube.

"In case you're wondering, it's a pierceless prince's wand. It seems appropriate, don't you think?" She looks up at me, smiling with lust in her eyes.

I shake my head violently, my heart racing as she repositions herself to gain better access to my cock.

When I start grunting in rage, she gives me a compassionate look. "Yes, it will be intense, but I want you to give in to it and enjoy it. That will be your submission to me."

I make a low, guttural sound deep within my chest as she places the tip of the instrument against the small opening of my penis. In a desperate attempt to stop her, I buck my hips hard.

The instrument flies out of her hand and I hear the metallic sound of it bouncing against the floor.

She frowns at me. "Do you realize how close you were to permanently damaging your cock? Don't pull that on me again or we could be heading to the ER."

A sense of dread washes over me as I watch her carefully clean it off and sterilize the instrument again before covering it in a fresh coat of lubricant.

"Stop glaring," she admonishes. "You're only allowed to look at your Mistress when I command it."

Samantha takes another shot of tequila before walking over to the cabinet to grab a blindfold. In a cowardly move, she covers my eyes.

Bitch.

"The blindfold will help you to concentrate on the intense sensations," she claims, trying to explain away her cowardice.

I feel the bed shift again as she moves into position.

I know there is nothing I can do to stop this—just like the lashes of my father's whip when I was a boy.

A chill travels down my spine as she presses the tip of the steel instrument against the opening and begins pushing it into my cock. I choose not to react as the hard metal spreads the opening of my urethra and slowly enters my shaft.

Samantha's breath quickens. "Oh God, I love watching it disappear inside you." She stops her progress for a moment and the bed shakes vigorously while she plays with herself.

After coming she murmurs, while pushing it in farther, "You are offering yourself in such an intimate way, Rytsar… I'm truly moved by your submission."

The feeling of being violated is more than I can bear, and I cry out against my gag.

My beautiful Tatianna suddenly flashes in my mind, but instead of smiling, she is screaming in pain. It's as if I'm carried back in time, and I watch the tortured expression on her face when she cries out the moment the first slaver savagely rips her virginity from her.

Tears run down the material of my blindfold as I personally experience a taste of what Tatianna was subjected to. My chest feels as if it will cave in from the heavy weight of my sorrow as I endure her violation at the same time as I experience my own.

In the ether of this strange netherworld, forces collide, and Tatianna and I meld into one another, connected by this horrific moment.

I wrap my arms protectively around her small frame

as the slaver continues to thrust into her and Samantha continues to push her instrument into me.

I cannot stop what is happening, my beautiful sparrow, I murmur to Tatianna, *but I'm here.*

I am here with you now.

My Comrade

Mercifully, I lose consciousness, but am forced back to reality when I feel the wicked tails of my 'nines rain down on my skin. I tense, a natural reaction to any painful stimuli, but soon relax under the fiery bite of the lashes, knowing I can't fight them.

"That's right, my handsome Russian…" Samantha coos above me. "Relax so you can embrace the pain of your cat o' nines."

She has no right to touch my 'nines—much less use it on me. But rather than give her the satisfaction of a response, I hold back my screams of fury as she continues to strike me haphazardly with the whip, oblivious to the safe zones of impact.

I feel the sting as my blood begins to ooze from multiple lacerations.

Holding my breath, I tense when she finally lays the whip down and grabs my shaft again.

"Your cock looks so sexy bound in the metal like this." She begins moving her hand up and down the length of my dick as she squeezes my balls with her other hand. "I can feel the prince's wand inside your cock, Rytsar. Do you like the feel of it when I stroke you like this?"

I make no sound, remaining completely still as I endure it, but she deludes herself into believing she has won over my submission.

"Your Mistress is pleased to see you finally embracing my dominance," she states with confidence.

Leaning over my head, her breast touches my cheek as she slowly unties the blindfold. Her confident smile quickly fades when our eyes meet, and she confronts the all-consuming rage I feel.

My gaze burns into her soul, my hatred for her is as palpable as a living beast in the room.

Samantha pulls away from me, her countenance suddenly changing to one of horrified shock. It's as if she has only now just realized the extent of her abuse.

She looks down at my body covered in the bloody marks she has created, staring at the wounds as if seeing them for the first time.

"Oh, my God, what have I done…?" she whimpers, her hand shaking as she brings it to her mouth and gets up. She stumbles backwards, a terrified look on her face.

Some guy runs by my room, shouting drunkenly just outside in the hallway. Samantha turns toward that sound with a look of sheer panic.

Without another word, she unlocks the door and opens it slowly. Taking a quick peek, she slips out, shutting the door behind her—leaving me alone in this state.

Tears of rage roll down my cheeks as I unsuccessfully struggle to loosen the ropes around my wrists. I am stuck here, bound to my own fucking bed, my cock aching with that hellish instrument still inside me, as my blood slowly drips from my skin onto the sheets.

I have never felt so helpless…

The longer I lay there, the darker my thoughts go. Soon the loathing I feel toward Samantha slowly reverts to myself. The degradation of what I've suffered begins to smother me, engulfing me in its dark embrace.

I cannot bear this shame.

There is a light rap, and I glance down at the crack under the door, seeing the shadow of someone standing there.

My heart skips a beat knowing the door is unlocked.

I can't let one of my college buddies catch me in this compromising position, so I hold my breath, silently commanding the person to leave.

"Durov…I know it's an ungodly hour, but I need to talk."

Thane! Relief floods through me. He is the *only* person I can bear to witness this humiliation.

With the ball gag still wedged in my mouth, I scream against it, praying he will be able to hear me.

I watch his feet shift, as if he's about to leave. Screaming for all I'm worth, I start pounding my head against the pillow, causing the bed to creak and rattle.

My eyes are riveted on the door as I watch the knob slowly turn. The door swings open, and Thane's jaw drops the instant he lays eyes on me.

Reacting quickly, he shuts the door behind him and

runs to the bed, unbuckling the gag.

"Oh, my God, Durov. Who did this to you?"

Bile crawls up my throat, demanding release. The instant I am free of the gag, I turn my head to the side and throw up.

Thane hurries to unbind my wrists and ankles, before heading to my private bathroom to get towels. "Let me get you out of that bed."

With his support, he helps me off the bed and leads me to a chair where he carefully begins to clean me off.

I have to lean against him, too weak even to sit up on my own, while I watch him attend to my numerous gashes in silence.

He works with gentle hands, even though he growls under his breath, "Who could do such a thing?"

I don't answer, looking down at my throbbing cock instead—I need to get that thing out of me. I make several failed attempts, trying to get the damn cock ring over the head of my shaft, but my hands shake too much.

In a quiet voice, Thane says, "Let me help."

I close my eyes, gritting my teeth painfully, as he eases the metal ring over the swollen head of my cock, then slowly pulls the long rod out.

I groan in relief once it's out and grab the cursed thing from him, throwing it across the room.

"Who did this to you?" Thane demands again.

Consumed with shame, I finally voice her name aloud. "Samantha."

Thane stares back at me, all color draining from his face. Before he starts asking questions, I tell him, "I never want to speak of it."

I try to stand up, but my knees buckle underneath me, and I collapse back into the chair.

"Stay where you are," he orders.

Unable to move, I watch helplessly as he strips the bed, throwing the linens into a pile. He then picks up the hated instrument and adds it to the pile, along with the dirty towels.

"Throw away everything she laid out. I don't want to keep anything she's touched."

When Thane picks up my 'nines, he looks at me questioningly.

As much as it pains me, I am resolute. "It's been ruined by her taint. Throw it out with the rest of the garbage."

He adds my beloved whip to the growing pile—giving me one more reason to hate Samantha.

After finding the extra set of sheets in my closet, he quickly makes the bed and helps me back into it. Going through my BDSM equipment, he finds a jar of salve and starts covering my wounds.

Thane says nothing, honoring my wish not to speak of it, but I see the building anger in his eyes as he quietly works on the gashes.

Once he's finished, he puts the salve away and states, "Samantha must be held accountable for what she's done."

"Do nothing," I insist.

Thane sits back on the edge of the bed, his face unreadable as he studies every scratch, bruise, and open wound on my body, as if cataloguing them in his head.

Finally, he informs me, "I have to confront her, but I can't leave you here alone."

I snort in disgust. "She did."

His eyes cloud over with guilt—a guilt he should not carry.

This is entirely on her.

"I'm going to get Anderson."

"*Nyet!*" I protest, sitting up in the bed.

Laying his hand on my shoulder, Thane pushes me back down. "You need strong people by your side right now."

"I don't want anyone else to know," I growl.

"You can trust Anderson."

I shake my head, not wanting the cowboy to witness my shame.

"Durov, I can't leave you alone, but I have to confront her—tonight. As her mentor, I'm responsible."

"This has nothing to do with you," I snarl angrily.

"I have to find out why she did this to you. I can't fathom the reason behind this attack."

"I suspect alcohol fueled her session of abuse, but I told her repeatedly to stop and called my safeword."

Samantha is in for an ugly awakening when the liquor wears off…and I am glad for it. I hope what she's done fucking haunts her for the rest of her life.

I nod toward the closet. "Go ahead and get Anderson but throw me a long sleeve shirt. He doesn't need to see the extent of what I've suffered."

As Thane hands me the shirt, he confesses, "I regret I didn't go out with you tonight."

"You weren't invited," I remind him. "I knew you

would never survive a night drinking with a bunch of Russians."

"Perhaps…" He nods curtly, but it's clear he still blames himself for what happened.

"I will dispose of these," he says, tying up the pile of discards in the sheet.

I watch with regret as he leaves the room, knowing another chapter of my life has ended.

I will never be the same after this.

Glancing around the room, I feel a sense of profound sorrow wash over me. I don't know how I will survive this…

Thankfully, Thane returns with Anderson not long after.

Anderson is clearly distraught when he enters the room and immediately blurts, "I'm sorry, man. I didn't even question leaving you with her." He shakes his head. "As a friend, I should have taken you up to your room myself."

"I'm not a child," I huff in irritation. "I told you to leave us. Had you tried to walk me to my room, I would have punched you in the face."

Anderson meets my gaze and vows, "I won't make that mistake again, even if you sock me in the face."

I chuckle in response, but it sounds as hollow as I feel.

Anderson fishes out a package from the backpack he's brought. "Knowing you, I bet you haven't had anything but vodka and pickles all night, so I brought you soup."

I look at Thane warily.

He grins. "Trust me. You're in good hands."

An involuntary shudder goes through me, my nerves suffering the aftershocks of the pain that Samantha has subjected me to.

Outside the door, I can hear the dorm coming back to life as the revelers return home after a wild night of celebration.

I've never felt this emotionally or physically raw before. I am profoundly grateful that Anderson is here to act as my shield against the world.

Glancing at Thane, I tell him. "Go. There is no need to stay."

Thane nods, then asks, "Is there anything you want me to say to her?"

"*Nyet*. She is dead to me."

I do not know how the guy does it, but Anderson gets me to eat two bowls of his Japanese ramen. Soon after consuming the last spoonful of spicy broth, my eyelids become sluggish and heavy.

To Anderson's credit, he doesn't question me about what happened with Samantha, choosing instead to tell me about his humorous family and their ranch, allowing me to fall asleep to the sound of his low voice.

After surviving the hellish night, my body drags me into a deep slumber I can't escape, and I sleep like the dead until late into the next morning.

When my eyes finally flutter open, I find Thane

watching over me and feel momentarily disoriented.

"How are you?" he asks with concern.

As the fog of sleep slowly lifts, it all comes back to me. Shaking my head, I sit up slowly and croak through a dry throat, "It's hard to tell."

Thane hands me a cup of coffee. "I got you this from the café. It's still hot."

I take the insulated cup, sipping the black coffee. It burns pleasantly on the way down, soothing my ragged soul.

I pull the sheet off and find my entire body is covered in dark bruises.

"You look worse than you did last night," Thane says, worry coloring his normally calm voice. "Do you need to see a doctor?"

I look at him as if he's crazy. "Of course not! There is no way I am answering questions about how this happened." I growl angrily, a fresh wave of humiliation washing over me.

"Still…you may need medical attention."

I throw the sheet back over my body to hide it from his gaze. "It'll be fine. I'm fine."

Thane states somberly, "I think you should press charges against Samantha."

"That will never happen."

"Why? This is clearly assault. Why protect her?"

"I am not protecting her. I'm protecting myself," I explain. "I don't want people to know about this. As far as I am concerned, it never happened." I turn away from him in shame.

I feel Thane's hand on me.

"But it did, Anton. This is not something you can forget, and she *needs* to be held accountable by the law and punished for her actions."

I turn back to meet his gaze, my eyes narrowing in irritation. "If I go to the police, I will be the one punished, don't you understand? All the details would become public knowledge. Not only would I be a laughingstock here in America, but everything that happened would get back to my family. *No one* can know!"

"Are you planning to confront her yourself?"

I wrinkle my nose in an angry snarl. "If I see her, I will kill her."

Thane suddenly looks troubled.

"I won't," I assure him. "As much as I want Samantha to pay, I don't want her dead." Shaking my head in disbelief, I admit out loud, "I cared for that woman…genuinely cared for her."

Then I growl in disgust, asking him, "How I could I possibly fall for a woman capable of this? What is wrong with me?"

His eyes flash with anger. "Nothing is wrong with you. No one knew what she was capable of—not even her."

"So, you spoke to her last night," I state, rather than ask.

"I did."

The assault is still too fresh to go over the details with him, but I *need* to know why. "What did you find out?"

"When I got to her dorm room, I found Samantha

huddled in a corner, babbling to herself."

I take small comfort knowing she's suffering. I want Samantha to drown in her guilt.

"What did she say when you confronted her?"

Thane sighs before answering. "She was in shock, unable to reconcile what she had done to you."

I snort in anger. "I told her to stop between my bouts of blacking out. She has no excuse for what happened."

"I agree," Thane states emphatically. "And I did not allow her to give me any excuses."

I glance at him, finally asking the only question I need answered. "Why? Why the fuck did she do it?"

"After hours of talking to her, I believe it boils down to a need to prove herself as a Domme to you, and a desire to give you the same life-changing experience you gave her."

"Well, she fucking changed it," I snarl, spitting to the floor.

Thane looks at me with compassion.

But I warn him, "If she comes anywhere near me, I will snap."

"I understand and told her that under no circumstances was she to contact you."

I can feel the rage building as images from last night replay in my head. Tears of fury roll down my cheeks. "No one can understand the betrayal unless they've experienced it." I swipe away the tears, my voice ragged when I tell him, "I never truly understood what Tatianna went through. Sure, I understood it on an intellectual level, but not on an emotional level. It makes what happened to her even more horrifying to me now."

I turn away from him, ashamed that I wasn't able to protect her from it.

"Tatianna should never have known such pain," Thane says with empathy. "No one should."

"She couldn't survive it," I cry out, my voice cracking with emotion, remembering my beautiful Tatianna lying on the floor in a pool of her own blood.

Thane puts his arm around me in support. "We can't change the past, but you and I *can* impact the future."

Even though his words resonate in my soul, I reject them. The pain is far too great to imagine a future.

The anguish continues to build up inside me until it reaches an unbearable level and I suddenly let out a primal scream—a long, loud cry of agony—releasing the pain and humiliation I feel.

Seconds later, someone raps hard on the door. "Everything okay in there, Durov?"

Thane speaks for me. "He's just letting out the frustration after a rough semester."

"Well, tell him to cut it out. It scared the crap out of me and I'm suffering from a killer hangover."

After he leaves, Thane tells me, "That scream didn't just scare him. It chilled me to the bone. I think it might help if you take a shower and let the hot water relax you."

Still shaking after my emotional release, it takes me a moment to respond. Moving stiffly, I get out of bed, feeling bruised and broken.

I turn on the shower and keep upping the heat, burning my skin with the scalding water in an attempt to wash away the feeling of defilement. But, no matter how hot the water gets, I still feel unclean.

After the water turns cold and I begin to shiver, I finally get out and dry myself off. Wiping away the steam left on the bathroom mirror, I stare at myself.

I don't recognize the hollow man looking back at me.

Walking out of the bathroom, I glance around the room. I can't remain here another second.

"Come with me to the beach house," I tell Thane.

"I can't, my friend. It would put you at risk."

"What are you talking about?"

"There's no need to concern yourself. You have enough to deal with right now."

I can sense his fear and want to help, welcoming the distraction from my own hell. "Tell me what's going on, comrade."

"No."

I put my hand on his shoulder and squeeze hard, insisting, "Tell me."

He lets out a tortured sigh before answering. "My mother has been transferred to the psych ward."

"She *is* crazy," I remind him.

"You don't understand. She's adept at manipulating the system. I guarantee she'll be out in six months—if she doesn't decide to escape first."

"Do not concern yourself. You have people who will protect you. I won't let her fuck with you again."

"I have no problem if she comes after me. I'm not afraid to take her to hell with me if needed." Thane shifts his feet, obviously uncomfortable about telling me what's truly bothering him.

Furrowing my brow, I demand, "What is it, then?"

Thane starts pacing the room, shaking his head. "This isn't the right time…"

I narrow my eyes. I'm in no mood to be played with.

Thane stares at me for a moment, then digs into his pocket and pulls out a piece of paper. "This was left under the door of my dorm."

I notice his hand is trembling as he hands it to me. A feeling of misgiving crawls over my skin as I open it and read the typed message.

The Russian is first.

I shake my head, staring at it. "What does this mean?"

"It's a threat from my mother. There's no other explanation."

I glance at the note again, feeling a perverse desire to face her. "You and Anderson will join me at the beach house," I state again.

"I'm a liability you don't need right now."

"*Nyet*, you are not. We are stronger together, comrade." When he says nothing in response, I press the issue. "Agreed?"

He nods, but I can sense he wants to run, believing it will save me.

Rather than give him that chance, I pack a bag and walk out with him, slamming the door on my dorm room—and the memories of last night.

Muffled curses echo from the nearby rooms in protest to the loud sound.

I escape down the stairs, wanting to leave unnoticed, but my friend Lucas stops me. "What the hell happened to you, Durov?"

I say nothing, but my heart starts beating faster and a cold sweat covers my body as the fear of discovery sets in.

"Hell, you look like you got hit by a Mack truck. How many shots *did* you drink last night?"

Realizing he thinks I'm suffering from a simple hangover; I force a smile. "I was the last Russian standing."

He punches me in the arm, not realizing he's just opened a wound. I grin wider to cover up the pain as I make my way toward the door, grateful I'm wearing a black shirt. "Next time, I'll invite you to join me and we'll see how many shots you can handle," I tell him as I head out.

"You do that, but we'll be drinking bourbon."

"Hah!" I laugh, walking out the door.

"You okay?" Thane asks when it closes behind us.

"I'll live."

I walk fast, not wanting to run into anyone else. I feel as if there is a neon sign over my head announcing that a woman assaulted me. I know it's irrational, but I can't shake the feeling.

When we arrive at Thane's building, I'm pleased to see Anderson has not left yet. "Get packing," I order.

He glances at Thane with a worried look. "What's happened? Where are we headed?"

"To my beach house," I answer.

Anderson slaps his hand against his thigh, grinning. "If that's the case, you don't have to tell me twice. I'm all for lounging on the beach. Best kind of medicine I know, other than the grandeur of my Rockies."

I dismiss myself while they pack, heading to the bathroom to dress my open wound in private.

Having been independent all my life, it surprises me how much I need these two. But what happened last night has shaken me to the core, and I don't trust myself to be alone right now.

I return to find them both packed and ready to go.

"Do you have any more of that soup?" I ask Anderson.

He smiles. "As a matter of fact, I do." Grabbing the last of his stock, he plops the few remaining packages into his duffle bag.

We head to my beach house in silence, both Thane and I too lost in our own thoughts to make light conversation. Thankfully, I feel the darkness start to lift as the blue expanse of the ocean opens up in front of us when I crest the last hill.

Anderson whistles. "Hell, yeah! That's what I'm talking about."

I nod in agreement, a smile coming to my lips.

Hopefully, this is what my soul needs to recover. At the very least, I'll be able to get a tan.

Power in Waves

The first thing I do when I enter the beach house is to strip out of my clothes and change into my swimming trunks. Grabbing a towel and a bottle of vodka, I head toward the door. "Meet you on the beach," I tell the others on my way out.

Anderson can't help but stare in shock at the multiple wounds on my body. When our eyes meet, he gathers himself and asks good-naturedly, "Hey, you want me to grab some glasses?"

I fight off the feeling of shame. "*Nyet*. Get your own bottle."

He chuckles, but I note Thane's concern as I walk past.

"Don't worry, comrade. I can handle my liquor."

I don't bother shutting the door as I leave, knowing the other two will soon follow. Dropping my towel and bottle on the sand, I head straight out into the water, needing to lose myself in the waves.

I'm lucky. The tide is especially high today, making

the waves crash violently into the shore.

Exactly what I need.

I'm desperate to release the rage burning inside me, and I welcome the fight against the powerful waves as I push myself out past the breaking point.

After a worthy battle, combatting the relentless power of the water, I finally make it out far enough to ride the large swells. I savor the sting of the salt invading each wound on my body, knowing it will help them to heal faster.

I try to relax as I tread water, determined to forget the events of yesterday even though memories of last night keep flashing in my head, tormenting me.

I hear splashing beside me and open my eyes to see Thane swimming up.

"What?" I growl, not wanting his pity or thoughtful advice.

"I was contemplating dunking you."

Now, that is something I can get behind. Without any warning, I dive down and swim toward Thane, going for his legs to pull him under the water.

He struggles, but he can't break free until I let go and we both swim to the surface gasping for breath.

"Never mess with a Durov," I laugh as he coughs up ocean water. I look to the shore and see Anderson is still on the beach. The last thing I want is for the guy to treat me differently because of what happened.

"What's up with the cattleman?" I complain.

Thane looks back at the shore and grins. "Nothing. He's decided to partake of your vodka while you're out swimming."

My eyes narrow in anger. "Like hell he will!"

I start swimming back to shore and suffer being pummeled by the waves again as I draw nearer to the beach. The violence of the water keeps forcing me into the sand time and time again until I finally make it to shore.

"Unhand the vodka, now!" I order as I approach.

Anderson lifts my bottle and grins before taking a swig, just to rile me up. I march over to him, glaring.

"Now, don't get your swim trunks all in a bunch," he teases, handing me the bottle.

I snatch it from him, making a point to wipe off the opening as if he's defiled it before I take a long draught, reclaiming it as mine.

Anderson looks me over and snorts. "Bloody Russian."

I look down at myself. Seeing my state, my lips slowly break into a smile. All my wounds have reopened and are bleeding because of my recent battle with the waves. I throw back my head and burst out laughing, appreciating Anderson's sense of humor.

I know I am with good friends because nothing has changed. Instead of treating me as if I am weak, both Thane and Anderson are giving me shit. I need that more than they know.

Handing him back the bottle, I declare, "For that, you deserve a shot."

Anderson winks as he takes a long swallow.

Thane has made it back to shore despite the harsh waves and walks up to us as I take the bottle back.

"I thought for sure you would have punched the guy

by now for daring to touch your vodka."

I look at Anderson with admiration. "A man who has the nerve to steal my vodka and then make fun of my bloody state deserves to drink with me."

Thane shakes his head at Anderson.

I take a long draught, savoring the vodka as it travels down my throat. Stretching out on my towel, I listen to the ocean waves with a genuine smile on my face.

The other two join me on either side and we lay sunning ourselves in silence. Being in the company of two people who can accept me without judgement puts me at ease—and the combo of fine vodka and California sunshine only adds to that feeling.

Turning my head toward Anderson, I ask, "What are your plans for the summer?"

"I'm headed back to Colorado in two days to spend the summer at the ranch. Our Kuvasz just had pups and I can't wait to hold them."

"I bet they're cute," Thane murmurs, soaking up the sun with his eyes closed.

I frown, turning my head toward Thane. "I thought you said you didn't like animals, comrade."

Thane opens his eyes and shrugs. "Bandit and Kiah are more like people in dog form—and almost as big."

"True," Anderson agrees.

I'm confused by Thane's sudden change of heart. He is not an animal lover any more than I am, so I call him on it. "I find it odd that you would say that when you have no use for pets."

"Well, I make an exception for those two. Besides, they're working dogs," he replies. Thane sighs in contentment as he basks in the warm rays of the sun.

I still can't fathom it and stare at him in disbelief.

"You'd love Kiah and Bandit," Anderson assures me. "And Bandit has a sadistic sense of humor like you," he says with pride.

"I may have to visit your ranch just to meet your dog *people.*"

"My family would welcome you," Anderson states amiably, but then adds, "However…if you touch any of my sisters, I will rip your heart out and eat it in front of you."

I laugh. "I like this side of you, cattleman."

Anderson props himself up on his elbows and stares at me. "You think I'm kidding?"

I laugh. "*Nyet.* I can tell you're a good brother and respect you for it more than you know."

He seems pacified by my answer and asks for a swig of my vodka. I hand it to him, and then pass it to Thane when he's finished.

"You're not planning on drinking me under the table, are you?" Thane asks before taking a sip.

My lips twitch in amusement. "It would not be a challenge, comrade."

He tips the bottle back and takes a long, Russian-worthy gulp of my vodka.

I raise an eyebrow, impressed by his determination. However, I don't believe for a second he'll last long against me, and I don't need him passing out so soon.

Enjoying his company, I take the vodka back without challenging him to drink more and chug a healthy portion myself. "Ahh…I enjoy the warmth of Russian vodka. It's like a blanket for my soul."

"I'm more of a whiskey man, myself," Anderson states. "Although, I never turn down a friend's liquor."

"Smart man," I answer.

We pass the bottle back and forth between the three of us until it's finished. By then I am experiencing a pleasant buzz. Taking in a deep breath, I let all the negativity out slowly.

For the time being, at least, I am okay.

"What about you, comrade? What are your plans for the summer?"

Thane glances at me with a hint of concern. "My uncle invited me to join him and my aunt on a two-month stint building houses for those affected by the Red River Flood."

I nod, having heard of the river that crested at fifty-four feet in Grand Forks and displaced tens of thousands of people. "A worthy endeavor."

"However, I don't have to go," he says quickly. "It's not like it's set in stone."

"It is important that you go." I state, not wanting Thane to worry about me.

"My uncle would understand if I chose to stay—no explanation necessary."

I shake my head. "If you have the opportunity to help others and connect with your own kin, do not pass it up."

"But you are important to me."

None of my four brothers has ever said that, much less my own father. I brush it off casually, not wanting either man to know about my difficult family history.

"Appreciated, comrade. However, family should come first—always."

Thane raises an eyebrow. "You are family to me."

My heart constricts, his declaration hurting me with its sincerity. I struggle not to react and fight back tears of gratitude. "Still, to shun your uncle's invitation would be a mistake, and it is for a good cause. I'll be fine."

Anderson pipes up. "Why not head back to Russia for the summer?"

Ice runs through my veins. Russia is the last place I want to be. I'm too raw to be around my own kin, and Tatianna's death is still too fresh. "*Nyet*. I have everything I need here. The sun, the ocean, and…"

I look down at my empty bottle of vodka with an exaggerated look of remorse.

Anderson takes the hint. "Hey, the least I can do is get you another one." He picks up the empty bottle and heads into the house.

I turn to Thane and tell him how I truly feel. "It will do my heart good, knowing you are following through with what you told me."

He frowns. "What do you mean?"

"You said you are dedicated to making a difference for the future. I can't think of a more appropriate summer endeavor for you." I discourage any further discussion by crossing my arms behind my head and closing my eyes. I soak up the sun's rays while I wait for Anderson to return with my vodka.

It takes Anderson far too long, but he eventually returns carrying a full bottle of vodka and three large coffee cups. "It's the best I could do," he apologizes as he hands each of us one of the mugs with a set of bamboo skewers with the ends cut off sticking out of each one. "I figured soup would be good here."

Thane chuckles, using the skewers as chopsticks as he slurps up a mouthful of noodles.

I follow suit, finding it humorous that I'm sitting on an American beach, consuming Japanese noodles with grilling skewers, while drinking Russian vodka. I never would have conjured up such a crazy mix on my own.

And, yet, it is exactly what I need.

The next morning, I stand beside the large, panoramic window facing the beach as the sun comes up in the east, coloring the wisps of clouds with its muted colors. I stare at a completely naked Anderson out by the shore and shake my head.

Thane comes up behind me. I watch Anderson scoop sand up in a shovel and toss the contents back into the ocean. "What the hell is the cattleman doing?" I ask.

He chuckles. "I think he's saving a starfish."

"In the nude?"

Thane smiles at me. "That's how the guy rolls."

I shake my head, thoroughly amused as we watch him in silence for over fifteen minutes before he suddenly looks up. When a jogger runs by, Anderson waves before scooping up another starfish.

Thane and I laugh as the jogger does a double take

before continuing on.

I like the man's fearless confidence. Although there are nudity laws in California, the guy clearly doesn't care.

He uses the shovel as a walking stick as he heads from the shore to the house, his impressive shaft swinging in the breeze.

"That's twenty starfish that will live to see another day," he announces proudly as he enters the house.

"And one traumatized jogger," Thane jokes.

Anderson grins in response. "Anyone who can't handle seeing a naked body needs to seriously look at themselves in the mirror."

We all laugh.

"After I take a shower, I'm making coffee. Anyone want a cup?"

"I'll take one," Thane answers.

"I'll stick to my vodka."

Once we're all seated at the kitchen table with our respective drinks, Anderson asks, "Do you mind if I am honest with you, Durov?"

"By all means. If I don't like what you say, I'll just punch you in the face."

He chuckles. "Well, at least I've been warned."

"*Da,* so ask away." I smirk.

He stares at me for several moments, his expression suddenly becoming serious. "I want you to know I stand behind you."

Tears unexpectedly come to my eyes. We've avoided the topic this entire time, and the first words out of his mouth on the subject completely undo me.

I let out a sigh. Unable to speak, I just nod my head.

"We both have your back," Thane adds.

Rather than get emotional in front of them, I suddenly challenge Anderson to an arm-wrestling match.

"You're on!" he replies enthusiastically, ripping off his fresh t-shirt and getting into position with his elbow on the table.

I like his zeal and sit opposite him, smirking as I grasp his hand. "Are you ready to lose, cattleman?"

"I think the question is…are you?" he states with confidence.

I have no doubt we are evenly matched, and I trust he will not let me win because of my injuries. The last thing I need is anyone's misplaced sympathy.

I squeeze his hand tight and tell Thane to count us down.

He stands beside us and calls out slowly, "Three…two…one."

I stare at Anderson, looking for any weakness as I focus my energy into forcing his arm down on the table.

I can tell he's as determined as I am, and it isn't long before we are both sweating from the strain of our muscles. But there is no way I'm losing this match. So, I push harder.

Anderson grunts in response, lowering his head as he concentrates on matching my strength.

I feel him start to give and am certain the match is over. That's when he lifts his head and meets my gaze, a twinkle in his eye.

Before I have time to react, the back of my hand slaps against the table.

I stare at him in shock, unable to believe he's beaten

me so soundly. With sweat pouring down my face, I sit back and huff. "I'm not used to being beaten."

"Do you have something to say to me?" he asks with a grin.

I frown.

"Something like, 'You, Brad Anderson, are the champion.'"

"*Nyet.*"

"Come on. Don't be a sore loser," he teases.

My lips twitch. "You *do* like to push my buttons, cattleman."

"You know you love me for it." His grin growing wider.

If the guy weren't so amiable, I'd sock him in the jaw. Instead, I mutter under my breath, "Anderson, you are the champion."

He chuckles. "See? That wasn't so hard, now, was it?"

I shake my head and down some more vodka.

Anderson winks at me, confessing with pride, "What I failed to mention is that I was the champion arm wrestler amongst the bull riders I traveled with on the circuits. You never stood a chance."

The guy has no shame, but he's right. It's part of the reason I like the fucker.

Anderson swipes the sweat from his brow and repositions himself. "Ready for another round?"

"I will decide when we have a rematch," I insist.

Anderson shrugs. "Suit yourself." He stands up, flexing to make his chest muscles dance.

I roll my eyes, turning to Thane. "Where did you find

this misfit?"

"Same place I found you."

I laugh, lightly slapping Thane's left cheek in rapid succession for his insolence.

Wiping the sweat from my brow with my forearm, I smile with satisfaction, having enjoyed the excursion of the wrestling match. Turning to Anderson, I ask, "So, what are the plans for today?"

"I've got to head back to the dorm and start packing if I'm going to get out of here tomorrow."

I glance at Thane. "And you, comrade?"

"Unfortunately, I need to pack, as well."

I'm disheartened to learn neither of them is staying, but I take it all in stride. "That's a pity as my only plans are to lounge on the beach and not pack a damn thing." I take a swig of vodka. "Here's to a productive summer for you both."

"What are your plans?" Thane asks.

"Simple. Beach plus vodka equals one happy Russian."

Blood Bond

Three weeks later, long after they've left, I'm now coming to realize I was only fooling myself.

I'm barely surviving.

Smothered in a fog of depression I can't get past; I have lost all sense of who I am…

Afraid of nothing before, I now dread each night as I lay down to sleep, knowing that once I close my eyes I will be ravaged by the demons in my nightmares.

They swirl around me, constantly calling out my name, beckoning me to follow them.

Thane insists the future is worth fighting for, but I disagree. Tatianna waits for me on the other side and I hunger to be with her again.

In an attempt to fight the insistent urge to end my life, I seek escape, inviting my Russian friends to join me at the beach house. The more chaotic the gathering, the better for me—anything to distract me from the darkness consuming my thoughts.

But…

It isn't working.

After trying to drink myself to oblivion every night, I find myself becoming immune to the effects of my beloved vodka.

I have no escape now.

Although I laugh louder than anyone else in the room, my soul is dying inside.

In the middle of one of these epic parties, my demons finally win. I slip pass my drunken friends and head down to the beach.

The waves call to me and I accept their invitation.

Completely dressed, I dive into the cold ocean water while the sounds of the party continue on behind me. Heading out to the open ocean, I swim until I have no strength left.

It's then, floating on my back and being gently rocked by the waves, that I look up at the stars above me and wait to join my Tatianna.

Peace.

When an image of my mother wailing over my grave unexpectedly clouds my vision, my heart starts racing. My mother has suffered unspeakable cruelty under the hands of my father, and she does not deserve to lose her son this way.

Mamulya will never forgive herself if I commit suicide—I know this.

I turn toward the shore and begin swimming, but panic sets in when it becomes obvious I can't make it back on my own strength.

A tingling chill of fear courses through me at the realization that it's too late…

Too tired to take another stroke, I tread water and look up at the stars, crying out, "I'm sorry, *Mamulya*. You deserved a stronger man for a son."

Guilt washes over me as a deep sadness replaces my fight to survive. My mother will never know I died trying to live.

"Rytsar!"

I jerk my head around in the water, startled. I swear I've just heard a young woman cry my name right next to me. The clarity of her voice is just as real as my own.

The desperation in her voice fills me with a surge of energy that builds in the core of my being and I look toward the beach again. Determined not to fail, I start swimming toward the shore.

Stroke after painful stroke, my muscles raging with fire from the sheer effort while my lungs burn with each breath, I inch my way to safety.

Before I make it to land, my body finally gives out. Letting out a cry of frustration, I slowly sink under the water.

"Daddy, is he dead?"

I open my eyes slowly.

The sun blinds me as I look up at the shadowy forms standing over me. Blinking, it takes a few seconds for my eyes to adjust to the sunlight.

The man bends down, laying his hand on me. "Are you okay?"

I nod, swallowing hard before answering. "*Da*…okay," I assure him, my voice gruff after taking in so much saltwater. I roll onto my stomach so I can slowly pull myself to my feet.

Apparently, my claim is not that convincing, because he immediately asks, "Do you need me to call an ambulance?"

"*Nyet.*"

He looks at me strangely. Realizing that he doesn't understand Russian, I force a smirk as I lie, "Too much to drink."

"Ah…" He steps back and wraps his arm around his son protectively. Glancing down at the boy, he adds, "You should drink more responsibly next time."

Taking his child's small hand, he gently scolds his son for staring back at me when they turn to walk away.

I look up at the sky, grief ripping at my heart.

I am not dead.

Instead of release, I must endure another day among the living. I kiss two fingertips and hold them up to the sky. "Only for you, *Mamulya*."

With a renewed sense of duty, I head back to the beach house, mentally preparing myself for the torture of a new day.

Adding insult to injury, I receive an impersonal letter at the end of the summer from my father, informing me that he has stopped payment on the beach rental, and I must return to the campus dorm.

I refuse to live in the room where I was assaulted and momentarily consider returning to Russia. However, I'm sure my mother would sense there is something seriously wrong and she can *never* know what happened here.

Desperate to keep my sanity, I strike a deal with a college mate to switch rooms, exchanging my spacious one for his much smaller one. A fair trade, in my mind—anything to keep the memories of that night far from me.

I lock up the beach house for the last time, groaning as I turn the key. It can no longer act as my refuge because of my father.

But it may be for the best, I concede.

The call of the ocean has become far too enticing for me to trust myself here any longer.

Being back on campus means I must actively avoid Thane. Just like my mother, I know he'll sense the depth of my inner struggle.

It's bad enough that he blames himself for bringing Samantha into my life, but if he were to discover how dark my thoughts go now, I'm unsure if he would be able to forgive himself. So, instead of causing him further pain, I avoid him at all costs for the first few weeks of the new school year by making excuses I know he will not question.

Despite my best efforts to elude him, however, Thane ambushes me while I'm heading to my economics class.

"We need to talk, Durov."

I don't even glance his way, purposely avoiding eye contact as I grumble under my breath, "I'm late, comrade."

Thane grabs my shoulder and whips me around, his gaze steady and unyielding. "I don't care."

Rather than make a scene, I smile and laugh it off. "What? Do you want me to skip class so I can drink you under the table?"

Thane cocks his head. "That might not be a bad idea."

I laugh for real this time. "*You* drinking vodka with me in the middle of the day instead of going to class?"

He shrugs. "You know what they say. You only live once."

I slap him on the back. I'm not in the mood to suffer through class, so I take him up on this rare offer to play hooky.

We head to my new dorm room and I usher him inside.

"I see you've downgraded," he states offhandedly.

"My father cut off funding, but I'm finding that less is more."

He looks at me with concern. "Is everything okay with your family?"

I shrug. "I suspect my father is simply asserting his power. So, *da*, everything is fine."

As he glances around the room, I suspect Thane understands the real reason I could not return to my original dorm room. Rather than question me on it, he looks at his watch. "It may be ten in the morning here, but it's six PM in London. Give me a shot."

I like his tenacity and grab two shot glasses out of my cabinet, along with a bottle of my best vodka. If I'm going to drink him under the table, it has to be with the best Russia has to offer.

"You seem reckless today, comrade," I comment, handing him one of the glasses.

He raises an eyebrow as he stares at it. "Isn't that a heavy pour, even for a Russian?"

I smirk. "*Nyet.*"

I grab a jar of pickles from my stash and open the lid, holding the jar out to him. He gingerly takes one and stares at the pickle dripping with brine.

I grin as I pull one out for myself and set the jar on the table. "Here's to my American friend getting his ass kicked in our first drinking challenge."

Thane chuckles. "We'll see about that…"

Throwing back the smooth fire, I groan with pleasure as the vodka goes down, enjoying a bite of the salty pickle afterward.

I watch in amusement as he chugs his own shot, coughing once before eating half his pickle. The guy doesn't stand a chance against me.

I pour us another shot, snorting as I clink my glass against his and then down it, finishing off the pickle. "Keep up, comrade! We're just getting started."

He nods in acknowledgement, swallowing it all before quickly consuming the last of his pickle.

I immediately pour us another, impressed that he's game for the challenge. "You know, you have no possibility of winning, but I admire your resolve."

"Just hand me the pickle jar," Thane insists, fishing out another one and chewing on it thoughtfully as he looks at me. Out of the blue, he states, "International

Women's Day is coming up."

A cold chill runs through my veins at the mention of the holiday. "So?" I try to hide the dark memories he's just stirred up with that statement.

"I'm wondering what your plans are for the day."

My heart suddenly hurts like a mother fucker as I relive the moment when I dropped the yellow flowers in my hand after seeing my beautiful Tatianna's lifeless body.

"I survive the day, comrade. I do not *plan* for it," I snarl resentfully.

"I was thinking…" Thane states, pouring us each another drink. "…maybe we should visit a church and offer up a prayer for Tatianna on that day."

"What?" I roar, furious at Thane for making such a presumptuous suggestion about something so personal. "You don't even believe in God, *mudak!*"

He hands my glass to me. "There's no reason to get belligerent. I know your faith is important to you, and I'm offering to join you as a friend."

"Do *not* force yourself on me," I warn him, full of unbridled hostility.

As if he hasn't heard me, Thane clinks his glass against mine before sucking down the vodka shot, slamming the glass on the desk when he is done. "You are hurting, Anton. I can see it as clear as day, and I'm not the type of person to ignore it, no matter how hard you push me away."

I snort in anger as I down my own shot, shaking my head violently when the image of Tatianna's white, blood-drained face flashes in my mind—those beautiful eyes staring lifelessly ahead…

"I'm tired of surviving," I unwillingly confess, the liquor breaking down my emotional walls.

No wonder he insisted on taking me up on my offer to drink…

I look at Thane with new understanding. I'd momentarily forgotten how smart he is, and I realize now that I'm in trouble.

"Each day you survive leads you to your new future, my friend," he insists.

"I no longer can bear it," I growl at him, unwanted tears forming in my eyes. "Everything I knew myself to be has been stripped away…" I turn from him. "I am no longer a man."

"You are wrong!" he insists. "You're still the same man you were before this happened."

"*Nyet*," I tell him, shaking my head. "I grew up believing I was strong and able to conquer the world. But now I understand my truth." I feel nauseated when I admit the ugly reality of my situation. "I am, and will forever be, a whipping boy."

Thane reacts as if he's suffered a physical punch to his gut. "That is not true!"

"It is the truth," I reply with deadly calm.

He grabs me by the shoulders, his eyes flashing defiantly. "We determine our truth. No one else—not the world, not our circumstances, and definitely not those around us. *We* are in control."

"Are we?" I ask, already certain of the answer.

Thane snarls angrily. "I have lived my life holding onto that truth because, if I am wrong…" He pauses, shaking his head. "…if I am wrong, then there would be no point in continuing on."

"Exactly."

I see the horror in his eyes when he realizes that's how I truly feel.

"Suicide is not an option. It is *never* an option," he yells.

I shrug, unaffected by his anger. "Maybe for some it is."

My words seem to open a floodgate of intense emotions for Thane, and he glares at me with a deep-seated rage I haven't seen before. "You *cannot* let your mind go there."

I look him straight in the eye. "It already has. Multiple times. Do you not think I wanted to die when I found Tatianna drenched in her own blood? The only thing that has kept me here is my mother. I could not bear to cause her that kind of pain."

"Then why would you consider doing it now?" he demands.

Knowing my answer will hurt him, I answer anyway. "When people find out I was assaulted by a woman, I will become the laughingstock amongst my kin and a source of embarrassment for my mother."

"No one has to find out," Thane insists.

I chuckle sadly. "The truth will always find the light, no matter how fiercely we guard it."

I watch Thane close his eyes. By the expression on his face, I suspect he is reliving the death of his father and my heart grieves with him.

When he opens his eyes again, however, they are

filled with anger. "It is cruel to place that heavy burden on others."

I'm unapologetically blunt with him and ask, "What about your own father?"

That loaded question unleashes the dark demons raging inside him. Tears of fury stream down his face as he shouts, "I hate my father for what he did!"

Thane turns away from me, trying to keep his emotions in check. But, once freed, they cannot be contained.

I'm moved by the open anger that flows from him because I share similar feelings.

Reaching out, I wrap my muscular arm around him in support. "There, you have finally said it. I was wondering how long it would take."

He looks at me accusingly, embarrassed that he's voiced his hatred toward his father out loud.

However, I understand.

"Your father killed himself in front of you. How could you not be angry with him?"

He shrugs off my arm, not wanting my sympathy. I respect that and am not offended.

Walking to the window, needing to distance himself from me, Thane admits, "All this time, I have run from the fact that he committed suicide." Turning to face me, he asks, "Do you know why?"

"Because he was weak?"

It's an honest answer, but I can tell I've upset him. Watching him struggle to rein in his emotions, I fully expect he's about to let out his fury all over my sorry ass.

Instead, he shakes his head and confesses *his* truth. "I

live every day afraid that I will make that same choice."

Thane's answer utterly shocks me. "You are the strongest man I know."

His intense gaze makes my heart stop for a moment. "I've thought a lot about it. If we are simply products of our parents and circumstance, like you insist, then I have one of two paths ahead of me. I will either become a monster, or I will die by my own hands."

I stare back at Thane, speechless—his chilling pronouncement hovering in the air around us.

Growling, he adds, "I refuse to believe that. I choose a different path, but I have to fight to stay on it every damn…fucking…day."

I let out a long, heavy sigh, nodding in understanding.

"Therefore, *you* must choose a different path, my friend—despite what happened to Tatianna, and despite what happened here. I guarantee it will be a difficult fight, but I will be alongside you every step of the way."

I swallow hard, not wanting to face such an impossible future. "I don't know…"

"You must."

I shake my head, looking down at my wrists. "When Tatianna committed suicide, I felt as if my life was over. I had no idea it could get worse."

Thane walks over to me, placing his hand on my shoulder. "If I could take your pain, I would."

I look up at him and see the sincerity in his eyes. "I would never wish it on you, but I appreciate the heart behind your offer."

"So, you vow to fight?" he insists.

As much as I want to join my Tatianna, his conviction has awakened something fierce inside me. Because others have failed me in the past, I demand a show of loyalty from him.

"I will, comrade. If you perform the blood bond with me."

Without hesitation, he asks, "What does it entail?"

"It is a vow of brotherhood. We will promise our fidelity, protection, and comradeship to each other."

I see the spark of understanding in Thane's eye.

We both need this.

"If I agree, you vow not to leave this world until your appointed time?"

"*Da*," I answer with confidence. "I give you my solemn vow not to rush my appointment with Death." I shrug afterward, grinning. "Unless, of course, the shit really hits the fan."

"You've had enough shit to last a lifetime," he replies, slapping me on the back encouragingly. "I predict it'll be smooth sailing from here on out."

"I hope you are right," I chuckle sadly in answer, knowing it wouldn't take much to push me over the edge at this point.

Walking over to my large chest on the floor, I unlock it and lift the lid slowly, pulling out my beloved blade, which I've nicknamed Retribution.

Turning toward Thane, I hold it up for him to admire. "This will do."

He raises an eyebrow as he studies the sizeable knife.

"However, we cannot perform the ritual here," I inform him. "It must be done at a sacred place."

Thane seems surprised. "Do you mean like a church?"

"*Nyet*, but similar in nature."

Nodding, Thane answers, "Ah, then you must mean the ocean."

"*Da*. That will do."

Smiling at me, he says, "I know the perfect place. I've visited it many times since my father died."

"Even better," I reply wholeheartedly. "A place that has meaning for you is best." My heart starts racing, knowing this is something we were destined to do. "Tomorrow night, then?"

"No, tonight."

A grin spreads across my face. "I approve of your Russian-like tenacity."

"What else do we need?" he asks, glancing at the blade I hold in my hand.

I tick off the items to him as I proudly hold up Retribution and admire it.

Tonight, he and I will become brothers.

Thane drives up the coast and parks on the side of a road next to the coastline. I grab my duffle bag and we head down a path that leads to a small beach surrounded by protruding rocks.

"First, we make fire," I announce to him.

"Is that part of the ritual?"

"*Nyet,*" I grin.

Thane shrugs. "Fire it is, then."

I dig a fire pit while Thane gathers driftwood. I take out the lighter I've brought and coax the flames to life. Together, we build it up one piece of wood at a time until we have an impressive blaze going.

I close my eyes and smile. "There is something holy about the sound of a crackling fire while the waves crash in the background."

"I agree."

We sit down in the sand and stare at the flames for a long time, neither of us saying anything.

In this moment, I am at complete peace.

It is a wondrous feeling.

"Have you done this before?" Thane asks me.

I look at him with a somber expression. "Of course not, comrade. It is an extremely rare thing to find a brother in this life."

He nods, his voice catching slightly when he shares, "I never thought it was possible—to be honest."

I smile. "And yet, here we are."

"Indeed.'

"Do you have any reservations?" I ask.

Thane shakes his head. "Not at all."

"Good. Neither do I."

I unzip my duffle bag and lay out a white towel before placing my blade and a strip of cotton cloth on it.

When I am ready, I turn toward him and say in a solemn tone, "Thane Davis, I promise you my fidelity, protection, and comradeship."

He returns my gaze, stating, "I am honored to call you my brother. I promise you, Anton Durov, my fidelity, protection, and comradeship."

I nod my acceptance of his vow and pick up Retribution. "Tonight, you and I unite together with blood. This bond speaks to my undying loyalty to you and cannot be broken."

Placing the point of the blade against my wrist, I puncture my skin as I drag it slowly across. I let out a low grunt of satisfaction as I watch the blood start to flow.

Handing the blade to Thane, I wait.

Thane gazes at the blade with a look of reverence. "Tonight, we mix our blood as a symbol of our brotherhood. I vow to never leave your side." He looks at my wrist, then finds the exact area on his before cutting into his skin.

I take Retribution from him, admiring the bloody blade before plunging it into the sand. Picking up the strip of white cotton, I press my wrist against his and wrap both tightly together, asking for his help to tie it.

I smile as our mingled blood soaks through the cloth.

Now only inches apart in this bound position, we are forced to stare into each other's eyes. I see clearly how he is constantly swimming in an ocean of pain connected to his past, and I suspect he can see the same reflected in my own eyes.

But I feel differently now that I have someone fully invested in my life—a person who knows my dark secrets and is not afraid to confront them with me.

The love and respect I have for Thane is boundless. Putting my free hand on his shoulder, I grin. "Welcome to my world, brother."

Placing his unbound hand on my opposite shoulder, he smiles. "Together, you and I will be unstoppable."

"*Da…*"

For the first time since that horrible night, I experience a sense of real hope.

But I Love You

As Thane and I sit down at the cafeteria for a quick lunch, I complain to him. "Comrade, that woman will not leave me alone!" I spit angrily, tired of Samantha's unending attempts to speak with me.

"I don't know what's wrong with her." He sighs in exasperation. "I've told her repeatedly to avoid you at all costs."

"She's obsessed!" I snarl. "Even when I threaten her, she acts like a moth to the flame, heading toward the light and her own death." I frown, adding, "She fails to understand that I do not make idle threats."

The concern in Thane's eyes intensifies. "I've warned her multiple times, but I will warn her again."

"Something must be done *now,* or I guarantee it will get ugly."

Thane closes his eyes, the heavy weight of this burden ripping at his heart. I know he feels responsible for both of us, and that he is desperate to spare me further pain while still protecting Samantha's life.

Some might question why I haven't demanded Thane cut all ties with the woman, considering what she has done, but I have my reasons.

Samantha risked her life for Thane and helped to send his insane mother to jail. She remained true to Thane, even when she knew she would become a target.

I owe her for helping my brother.

She has also been working under his mentorship for months, learning the fundamentals of being a Dominant. Being an honorable man, Thane carries the shame and guilt of her actions that night, and I know he feels he failed her in some way.

Thane must find redemption.

But the main reason I don't want him cutting all contact with her is that I've come to understand Samantha on a deeper level. I know that behind that tough as nails exterior lies a little girl who feels unlovable and alone.

Her obsessive need to speak with me comes from a place of inner loathing and fear. A deep-seated fear of herself—and her own destructive nature.

I think she holds out hope that she can rejoin the pieces she shattered that night simply by sheer will. She has yet to accept that her actions killed any feelings I had for her.

Eventually reality will sink in and, when it does, she will not survive it without Thane by her side.

I told Thane that even though I want to wrap my hands around her skinny throat, I don't want her dead. While I can never forgive Samantha for what she has done, I don't want to live in a world where she no longer exists.

There has been enough sorrow in my life that I don't want to bear responsibility for her death as well. So, I have encouraged Thane to continue his friendship with her. If anyone can make a difference to that fucked-up bitch, I believe he can.

"What do you suggest, comrade?"

Thane looks at me as if he already knows my answer but makes the suggestion anyway. "Would you be willing to get a restraining order against her?"

I snort in disgust. "The police cannot be involved, you know that. Besides, it wouldn't stop her any more than it did your mother."

He sighs in resignation, hesitating for a moment before asking, "What if we had a controlled meeting? One where you hold all the cards? You decide when, where, and what is discussed."

"What would be the point of putting myself through that?" I growl.

"You will be able to rid her of any notion that forgiveness is an option."

I shake my head in disgust. "How do I know she will listen any better than she did that night?"

"For one, she'll be completely sober. And I will be there to witness the conversation so I can remind her of what you said should she ever question it in the future."

"Do you really think it will make a difference?" I ask him, still doubtful.

"If it doesn't, I'll insist she attend another college. Your sanity should not be put in jeopardy because of Samantha. This at least gives her a chance to stay if she is sincere in her remorse."

I state gravely, "Do you know what will happen if she is forced out?"

Thane nods, a pained look on his face.

We both know she won't survive it.

"But, again, she will have made that choice," he answers sadly.

"Very well. I will meet with her to end this once and for all."

Not a man to procrastinate, I set the meeting for the next day. I don't want to spend another minute of my life thinking about her.

To say I feel anxious as the hour of our meeting approaches is an understatement. I am highly agitated by the prospect of facing Samantha again and must calm my ravaged soul by thinking of my mother.

I will not be able to return to Russia if I were to go into berserker mode around Samantha. To compose myself, I slug a couple of shots of vodka just before the designated time.

I've chosen to meet her in the office building of a family friend who runs a successful trading company here in LA.

I sit down behind Pyotr Gagarin's massive desk, pleased with both the size of the furniture and the distance it will put between Samantha and I. The chairs facing the desk look miniscule by comparison—just the way I want it.

I stiffen when I hear the two of them outside in the hallway.

I look to the heavens and mutter, "God, I don't ask much of You, but I'm asking now. Give me the strength not to kill her."

I remain seated as the door swings open and Thane enters the office. He gives me a nod, silently asking if I'm still okay with Samantha entering the room.

Although I am not, I nod back, trusting that God will prevent me from strangling her.

Thane gestures to Samantha and I hold my breath as she walks in.

The bitch is as beautiful as ever, with her long blonde hair and those killer legs, but instead of feeling intense attraction toward her, I only feel vile loathing.

Before she can meet my gaze, I turn my attention on Thane. He is the only person who matters to me.

"Samantha appreciates you agreeing to meet with her," he states.

I huff in irritation, not bothering to look in Samantha's direction, but I can already feel my rage building due to her proximity.

"Yes, thank you," she echoes.

My eyes narrow as I turn my head and stare at her, growling ominously under my breath.

She immediately drops her gaze to the floor, noticeably trembling.

I sit back in my oversized chair, forcing myself to slow my breathing while my fury increases with every second that ticks by.

I haven't asked them to sit yet.

Realizing this is a mistake, I glance at Thane, ready to tell him so but he speaks first.

"Samantha has something she wishes to tell you."

Deciding to get it over with, I glare at her. "Out with it, then."

Samantha lifts her gaze, but the moment our eyes meet, she immediately falls to her knees. "I'm so sorry, Rytsar…"

"Never call me by that name again!" I howl, incensed that she would dare to use it.

Samantha's face crumbles in sorrow, but she nods meekly to indicate she understands. Taking a deep breath, she begins again. "I have no excuse for what happened. I know that. But…I am sorrier than you will ever know."

My eyes narrow as I grip the arms of the chair, not trusting myself to speak.

Her voice falters as she continues. "If I could take back…what happened, I would." She looks at me beseechingly. "I will do *anything* to make this right."

"There is nothing you can do," I state emphatically.

I watch her shiver when she hears the finality of my tone.

Tears come to her eyes. "Send me to jail. I'll willingly serve my time. But, please, don't forsake me."

I scowl at her, unmoved.

Her bottom lip quivers when she informs me, "I'm going to a counselor, and I just joined AA. I will never touch another drop, I promise." She glances at my comrade. "Thane even suggested I serve under an experienced Domme so I can learn by example."

I huff in disbelief. "*You* serving under another?"

She nods. "Yes, because I have no business being a Dominant until I understand the needs, desires, and struggles a sub faces."

I roll my eyes, not believing she is capable of being a fulltime submissive.

"I will do it. I give you my word," she declares.

"Why? Why do all that?" I demand, suspicious of her motives.

She swallows hard before answering. "I cannot give up BDSM now that I've tasted it, but I have to guarantee that what happened with you never happens again."

I huff angrily. "It should never have happened in the first place. I told you to stop numerous times!"

"I know," she whimpers, cowering under the intensity of my fury. "I'm devastated that I hurt you."

I glare at her in disgust. "You betrayed me on the deepest level a person can."

Tears fill her eyes as she chokes out, "I'm sorry. So deeply sorry."

"There can be no forgiveness—ever."

She shakes her head, not wanting to hear it. I glance at Thane with a look of *I told you so.*

He immediately speaks up, telling her, "Samantha, you didn't come here seeking forgiveness."

She closes her eyes and nods. "No, I did not."

I don't believe it and growl under my breath.

"Repeat what Durov just said," Thane commands.

Her voice catches when she says, "There can be no forgiveness…"

I say nothing, letting the minutes drag out uncomfortably for her. I want every second to be torture.

When Samantha can't take the silence any longer, she opens her eyes to meet my gaze.

"But I love you, Anton."

I stand up, balling my fists to prevent myself from jumping over the table and strangling her right then and there.

With finality, I tell her, "You are dead to me."

I hear her gasp as she crumples to the floor.

I look at Thane. "Get her out of here."

Turning my back on Samantha, I start counting, forcing myself not to move as rage consumes me.

I love you…

The words echo in my head as the pain and humiliation of that night comes rushing back, and I must clench my teeth to prevent myself from screaming.

How dare she make that declaration after what she's done?

Thane helps Samantha to her feet, and I can hear her quiet sobs as they walk out of the office.

The flood of adrenaline my anger has incited makes it difficult to keep still, so I conjure up a vision of my mother and continue counting slowly.

Relief flows through me when I hear the door close, followed by the hollow sound of Samantha's stilettos echoing down the hallway.

I've survived.

Opening the drawer of the desk, I pull out my vodka to celebrate.

Thane meets me later that night to check in with me. "How are you holding up?"

I sigh as I think back on the meeting. "As long as I never have to speak to her again, I will be fine."

"It's unfortunate that it required Samantha seeing you face to face for her to fully understand the extent of the damage she's done."

"What was up with that fucking declaration?"

Thane shakes his head. "I was shocked when she said it."

"You don't tell someone you've assaulted that you love them," I growl in disdain.

"No, but it does explain why she was determined to meet with you, despite our multiple warnings. She's been seriously deluding herself."

I frown, uncertain that the meeting had any lasting effect on her. "Do you think she understands now, comrade?"

He looks me in the eye. "The meeting today destroyed any illusions she had."

"At least I can hold onto that," I tell him.

I gaze up to the heavens. "I give thanks to God and my sweet *mamulya* that Samantha still walks among the living." I look back at Thane. "All those feelings came rushing back the moment she entered the room."

"I regret that you had to endure it, brother," he states sadly. "I wish I could have spared you."

"Knowing she's remorseful did help to hold my anger in check."

I stare hard at Thane. "I trust you will do everything necessary so no one else suffers under her hand. I would not be able to forgive myself if she assaulted another."

"I feel exactly the same way," Thane says, then vows, "I will be unfailingly vigilant."

I nod, knowing he will not fail me—or Samantha—and it gives me some semblance of peace.

Thane looks uneasy when he asks, "I've noticed that you haven't been to the dungeon for months. Why is that?"

I feel the knots in my stomach start to twist when I admit, "I am not the man I was, comrade."

"It's an essential part of who you are. I remember when you told me that BDSM takes the physical and mixes it with the spiritual so you can experience internal balance."

I grimace, haunted by my own words.

Thane looks me directly in the eye. "You need to experience that again, brother."

I shrug, growling like an angry cur. "It's not possible anymore."

"Why?"

"Without my 'nines, it feels as if my arm has been cut off."

"You can't think that way," he insists.

I frown, irritated that Thane is trying to tell *me* how I should think. "You have no idea what you are talking about."

"I disagree."

When I snarl under my breath in response, he smiles.

"Trust me. I know exactly what you need."

Putting his hands on both my shoulders, Thane turns me around and pushes me toward the door. I reluctantly follow as he leads me to his dorm building.

Once inside his room, I stand with my arms crossed and a scowl on my face as I watch him rummage through his closet.

My jaw drops when he produces my cat o' nines.

I never thought I would see my 'nines again and stare at her as if I'm seeing a ghost.

"I had to keep everything in case you decided to press charges against Samantha. When it became obvious that you weren't going to, I threw it all away," Thane explained. "However, I couldn't get rid of your cat o' nines. This instrument is a part of you, my friend. So, I cleaned it thoroughly several times, determined to make it as clean as the first day you wielded it."

Staring down at my 'nines with affection, I slowly hold out my hand to take it from him.

The instant I touch my tool, I feel the spark of connection. Tears flow freely when I tell him, "I'm indebted to you, *moy droog*."

He nods, smiling. "I knew you needed it."

I swing my 'nines for the first time in months. The muscles in my arm and back stretch as the wicked tails cut through the air and it suddenly feels as if I can breathe again.

Thane stares at me, his smile growing wider. "It's good to see you're back."

I sigh in pure pleasure as I swing her several more times.

"I think there is only one thing it's still lacking," Thane states.

I stop for a moment, tilting my head. "What is that, comrade?"

"It needs to be anointed with the grateful tears of a sub."

I nod my agreement, looking back at my 'nines. "That is exactly what she needs."

Thane glances at his watch. "Luckily, the dungeon is open right now. What do you say we head straight over there?"

"Have you eaten?" I ask when I hear his stomach growl.

"No. Have you?"

"*Nyet.*"

He reaches into a bag on his desk and tosses something at me. My reflexes automatically react, and I catch it before I know what it is. Looking down at my palm, I see a green apple.

"I'd like to fill up on scenes tonight rather than food," he explains.

I throw it into the air and catch it before taking a bite out of the tart fruit. With the juices still dripping from my lips, I nod. "I couldn't agree more, brother."

I'm surprised by my increasing anxiety when we arrive at the old warehouse that houses our secret BDSM club. Normally, I only feel a sense of relief as if I'm returning home—but not tonight.

I hesitate, having second thoughts about coming here. "This is a mistake."

" No, it is not," Thane assures me, pushing me toward the entrance. "This is exactly where you need to be."

I start to back away from the door. "I can't. I'm not that man anymore."

Thane stops me. "Do you remember when you told me what the key to being a Dominant is?"

I look at him, shaking my head.

He presses his hand against my chest. "Being a Dom comes from here, and the core of who you are hasn't changed."

I'm about to protest and insist he's wrong when I hear a squeal behind me.

"Oh, my goodness, it's Rytsar Superstar!"

I turn to see luna fall to the ground in a bow of supplication. "I'm sorry, Rytsar! It just flew out of my mouth before I could stop it. I know I must be punished."

Seeing her bowing before me ignites my dominant nature. Although I give her a look of disapproval, inside I am pleased.

Her enthusiastic greeting infuses me with confidence.

"Luna, we have spoken about this before," I scold her.

She presses her head to the pavement. "Yes, Rytsar." Her voice is ripe with guilt when she replies, "You told me never to call you that in your presence."

"So, you understand the reason you must be punished?"

"I do, Rytsar, and I gratefully submit."

Since punishment is expected, I cannot shirk my duty. However, I have already decided what exquisite torture I will make her endure before I deliver multiple orgasms she won't forget.

I appreciate the difference luna has unknowingly made for me tonight and will reward her for it—after I punish her.

With renewed confidence, I step up to the door and knock.

The guard on the other side asks, "What is the one truth?"

I look back at luna and smirk. "All is fair in passion and pain."

She drops her gaze, biting her lip in anticipation.

I nod to Thane; grateful he's pushed me to return here. Walking through the entrance, I head down the metal staircase to the basement. A woman cries out in pain on the other side of the heavy door, sending a pleasant jolt down my spine and hardening my cock.

Yes, this is exactly where I need to be.

I open the door and stride into the dungeon, taking in a deep breath as I savor the smell of sex, leather, excitement, and fear.

The room breaks out in excited chatter when I enter. Luna, it appears, is not the only one who has missed me.

Subs who are not exclusively collared start crowding around me, begging to be my first for the evening. I look down the line of submissives who wish to taste my 'nines again and my gaze lands on a curvy woman with a mass

I feel her tremble as fresh tears fall down her cheeks. She swipes them away hastily. "I don't normally cry. I'm sorry."

"Do not apologize. I happen to enjoy a sub's tears."

She smiles at me gratefully. "You aren't nearly as scary as people led me to believe."

Chuckling softly, I tell her, "Wait until you feel the caress of my 'nines, cee. I will introduce you to fear."

Her pupils grow wide, and she swallows hard again. "I can't wait."

"Undress for me," I command huskily.

I step back and start swinging my 'nines as I watch her strip. I purposefully observe cee as she undresses, not only to admire her body, but also to note which movements cause her the most pain.

Her courage is something I admire and can relate to. While hers is physical and mine is internal, the struggle is similar. To face excruciating pain every day and continue on…we are more alike than she knows.

She is a warrior and, today, I plan to treat her like one.

When she is completely naked, she stands before me, sighing softly under my gaze as I walk around her. Grunting my approval, I take in her feminine curves and the artistic tattoos that cover her body. I can sense that she is shy about being exposed but is brave enough to bare herself to me in front of the others in the dungeon.

That kind of mettle is as beautiful as that wild hair and her brown eyes, which shine so bright.

I hold out my instrument to her and command, "Kiss my 'nines in gratitude."

She looks up at me as she kisses it tenderly with those full lips.

Smiling at her, I start caressing her body with the leather tails of the cat o' nines. Goosebumps rise on her skin as she reacts to its gentle touch.

She knows it will soon demand more of her.

I drag the leather over her large breasts and watch in satisfaction as her nipples contract into hard buds. Taking my time, I acclimate her body to the gentle caress, noting how wet it makes her.

Swiping my hand between her legs, I make her cry out as I tease her clit with my vigorous rubbing. I could make her come right now, but I want to prolong her climax so that the release is all that much more intense.

Without giving her satisfaction, I command her to lift her arms and bind both wrists above her head, making sure to leave enough slack so her body won't be overly taxed in this position.

Moving back, I ask, "Are you ready, cee?"

She shivers in anticipation, answering with certainty in her voice, "Yes, Rytsar."

I like the way my name rolls off her tongue, and I smile as I deliver my first stroke.

Her cry of surprise is priceless.

"Color, cee?"

She pants out her answer. "Gr…een."

"Are you sure?" I ask, smirking.

Turning her head, she flashes a beautiful smile. "Ab-solutely."

I feed off her enthusiasm, testing her as I apply strokes of varying intensity. I purposely do not break the skin, only leaving beautiful red welts over her body.

I am not surprised to find that she has a strong pain tolerance. It allows me to take her farther than most subs new to my cat o' nines.

When I have her tearful and trembling, I lay my 'nines down and pick up my Magic Wand. Wrapping an arm around her, I growl in a low voice, "Come for me."

I turn on the Magic Wand and press it against her clit. Her body is so primed for release that she orgasms the moment the vibrating tool makes contact.

Cee cries out in ecstasy for all in the dungeon to hear.

I pull it away afterward and ask, "Would you like another?"

"Yes…" she murmurs breathlessly, flying on endorphins and the last pulses of her climax.

I press the vibrating wand against her swollen sex again and watch in satisfaction as her body is rocked by another powerful orgasm.

While she stands there swaying in her bonds, I step back to deliver another round of strokes with my 'nines. I cover her back with its painful caress, praising her as the tails of the instrument dance across her mottled skin.

This time, when I stop, I do not rely on a tool but my own touch to bring her to multiple orgasms. Her cries of passion resonate throughout the dungeon, making her the center of attention.

I'm certain I now have the other Doms questioning why they passed on her before, and I suspect several will be approaching her once the two of us are finished here.

But they will have to be patient, because I am not finished with her yet.

"Are you ready for your last round?"

She is slow to answer, flying on the waves of the sub high I've carefully crafted for her.

"Yes…Master of pain."

I smile to myself, liking that title.

Grateful for her trust and submission, I reward cee with challenging strokes that send her higher without breaking her subspace.

By the end of our session, she is completely drenched in sweat and tears, but that stunning smile does not leave her face, even after I free her from the bindings.

"My beautiful warrior sub," I say proudly as I help her to a nearby bench to sit.

She stares as me with half-lidded eyes and that charming smile. I can tell she wants to say something but is unable to form words just yet.

I wait, looking at her with genuine admiration. I know we needed each other tonight. In me, she found acceptance and blessed relief, while I have reclaimed my purpose.

In a world of constant pain, a sadist's skill has immense worth. My scene with cee has reminded me of that tonight.

I will not doubt myself again.

In a hoarse whisper, her throat raw from her screams of pleasure and pain, cee tells me with tears in her eyes, "You set me free."

I kiss her on the lips. "Your strength inspired me."

She shakes her head, and that shyness I saw earlier suddenly returns.

I lift her chin up. "*Da.*"

A red blush colors her cheeks.

I watch with pride as several Doms walk toward us, hoping to have an opportunity to speak with her.

I kiss her one last time. "You hold the power. Choose wisely, my warrior sub."

I leave cee, certain that she has cemented her place in this community as firmly as I have.

Seeking out Thane, I find him enjoying a spanking session with two enthusiastic subs. When he looks up momentarily and notices me, I give him a nod of thanks.

Thane smiles, his eyes flashing with the thrill that Dominance brings as he turns his attention back on the two subs eagerly awaiting pleasure at his hand.

I cross my arms in satisfaction, glancing around the dungeon, certain of my place in the world.

Nothing can shake me now.

The Submissive Training Center

Thane asks Anderson and me to meet him at the library, hinting that he has something extremely important to share.

When we arrive, Thane rushes over with a huge smile on his face "I was able to get an invitation for us to observe an auction at the Submissive Training Center."

"You're pulling my leg," Anderson grins, not taking him seriously. "That place is impossible to get into because of their extensive vetting process for Doms."

"You're right," Thane agrees. "However, we're going there purely as observers and have been granted special permission."

I scratch my chin, which is rough with stubble because I forgot to shave in the morning. "I'm impressed, *moy droog*. The school has quite the reputation, even in Russia. I've always been curious what the Center's elite submissives were like."

"I'm curious, as well," Thane agrees, his eyes flashing with excitement. "I've been interested in the inner workings of the school ever since I first heard about it from several of the Doms at the dungeon."

I understand Thane's attraction to the Training Center because he has a natural talent for teaching. Me, on the other hand? I'm simply interested in the submissives themselves.

"How exactly were you able to secure an invite for all three of us?" Anderson asks, clearly still doubting his claim.

Thane's enthusiasm is contagious when he answers, "You know what they say about being in the right place at the right time?"

"Sure…" Anderson says, encouraging him to continue.

"I happened to be waiting at the bus stop when an unusual couple sat down beside me. I couldn't help noticing she seemed overly intent on her partner. When I spied the thin collar around her neck, I suspected that it must be a D/s pairing. But it wasn't until he whispered, 'Straighten your back and keep your hand on me at all times,' that I realized I was witnessing a submissive in training.

"I'll admit I was intrigued and stared at them until the man called me on it by asking, 'Is there something I can help you with?'"

Thane chuckled. "I was caught off guard by the question and was more than a little embarrassed, but that feeling only intensified when I met the man's gaze." He shook his head, looking amused. "There is something definitely intense about Marquis Gray."

I feel as if I've heard that name before and ask,

"Who is he?"

Thane grins, his eyes glinting when he tells me, "Turns out I was speaking to a trainer at the Submissive Training Center, who happened to be out on a practicum with one of his students."

"No way!" Anderson exclaims.

"Can you believe it?" Thane seems more excited than I have ever seen him. "The two of us hit it off, so I shared my respect for what the school is doing for submissives, as well as my own curiosity about the program itself. Marquis Gray was interested in hearing my thoughts after observing one of their auctions and invited me to observe one."

Thane looks at us both and grins. "But what fun would that be if you two weren't there with me? So, I asked if he'd be willing to also invite the two men who've helped in my journey to become a Dominant."

"Well, that was ballsy of you," Anderson states with admiration, sweeping his hair back.

Thane shrugs modestly. "Get this. He was actually interested to hear that we were working together and mentioned the Training Center had started a new training program for Dominants just last year.

"You don't say…" Anderson responds, appearing more interested than ever.

Thane turns to me. "You're unusually quiet, Durov."

"I haven't seen you like this before, comrade. I'm finding it…amusing."

He smirks. "Glad I can entertain you."

"When is the auction?" I ask.

"Next Saturday. Needless to say, I'm hoping we get a

tour of the Training Center afterward."

"Wouldn't that be cool?" Anderson agrees.

Even though I have no interest in training a sub or the learning process behind it, I'm grateful to have an opportunity to peek inside the world-renowned school. I know that several of my fellow sadists back in Russia will be jealous when they hear that I've been.

Per Marquis Gray's instructions, we arrive at the school an hour before the auction begins. The school itself is a large brick building, but nothing of note to hint at what's happening inside.

Anderson seems to be in a particularly slaphappy mood and keeps elbowing me as we walk up to the entrance of the school. I give him a hearty shove and laugh when he loses his balance and almost hits the pavement. Thane gives us both an unamused look.

Despite our shenanigans, as soon as we walk through the doors, we drop our foolishness. Thane walks up to the information desk to speak with the receptionist. "Hello. We were invited to observe the auction today."

"Oh, yes. Marquis Gray informed me that you were coming. I'll let him know you're here." As she picks up the phone, a man behind us states, "No need, Ms. Dunningham."

The three of us turn around at the same time. In front of us stands a thin man with dark eyes and unusually pale skin. The thought crosses my mind that he might be a real live vampire, and I smile to myself.

"Does something amuse you?" he asks me.

For some odd reason, this man renders me mute, and I just shake my head.

He then turns his attention to Thane. "Welcome to the Submissive Training Center, Sir Davis. I take it these are the two gentlemen you spoke so highly of?"

Thane nods, seemingly as mute as I am. He quickly recovers, however, and introduces Anderson first. "This is my friend, Master Brad Anderson."

Marquis Gray holds his hand out to him. "A pleasure to meet a friend of Sir Davis."

Anderson shakes his hand vigorously. "The pleasure is mine, sir."

"You may call me Marquis Gray."

"Will do." Anderson glances at Thane for a moment, then suddenly clears his throat, becoming more serious. "I want to thank you for including me today."

The trainer smiles slightly. "You can thank your friend for that."

Anderson glances in my direction, giving me a nervous wink.

I'm dumbfounded. What it is about this man that has all of us off balance?

Thane turns to me next. "This is my other good friend Rytsar Durov."

I inadvertently hold my breath as I shake Marquis Gray's hand and meet his gaze.

He says nothing for several minutes, staring intently into my eyes, before asking, "Why are you here?"

I'm unsure why he's asking me that and say, "I

couldn't pass up the opportunity to observe an auction at the Center."

The man does not seem satisfied with my answer and asks again, "*Why* are you here?"

I shake my head, getting the uncomfortable feeling that he is asking something more profound than I'm prepared to answer.

Thane wasn't kidding about the man being intense!

I let out my breath slowly when he finally turns his attention back on Thane. "Let me show you the way."

Marquis Gray thanks the receptionist before leading us to the elevator. As he presses the button to the lower level, he explains, "You are only here to observe. We have an area set aside for you. Understand, you are not to interact with the vetted Doms nor with any of the submissives you might come in contact with."

I click my tongue in disappointment on hearing that the submissives are off limits, but then immediately regret it when his eyes return to me. "Do you have an issue with that, Rytsar Durov?"

"*Nyet.*"

The man nods, accepting my answer before ushering us into the open elevator.

I look up at the ceiling to avoid further eye contact with him. I'm used to making others feel intimidated in my presence, *not* the other way around.

I brave a glance at Thane, who appears to have a slight smile on his lips. Is he finding my discomfort amusing?

I chuckle under my breath, surprised to find myself in this odd situation.

Marquis's attention is back on me. "You seem to be either highly entertained or uneasy. Which is it?"

Suspecting the man won't let me be until I answer him, I tell him the truth. "It's the latter."

"Ah…" he states, saying nothing more.

I feel only relief when the doors open. I step out into a large commons area lined with college classrooms. At one end of the commons sits a temporary stage with a partition. I assume that's where the auction will take place.

Marquis Gray leads the three of us to the left side of the stage. "You will stand behind the line taped on the floor once the auction begins. We want you up close so that you can observe everything that takes place, but I must remind you again, you are not to speak to or interact with any of our guests. This is a courtesy to you. Do not abuse it."

Once we all agree, Marquis takes us back behind the partition and walks us over to a smaller man with a wiry frame.

"Mr. Gallant, these are the three I was telling you about."

The man is busy setting things up, but stops his work, breaking into a smile when he sees us.

The warmth of his smile instantly puts me at ease. Holding out his hand, he shakes each of ours, explaining, "I'm a teacher here—not to be confused with one of the trainers."

"What's the difference?" Anderson asks.

"Great question, Mr. Anderson," he replies, his smile widening. "I teach in a classroom." He points to a room where I can see a row of desks and a large whiteboard on the wall. "I cover the basics with the submissives, whereas a trainer like Marquis Gray actually works with the submissive during their practicums, where they can experience what we've talked about in class."

Thane speaks up. "Does that mean you don't physically train the submissives yourself?"

"That's correct."

"How many trainers are there per course?" Thane asks, clearly intrigued.

"We have four trainers on the panel."

"Why so many?" I ask, thinking it seems excessive to me.

Mr. Gallant's eyes flash with pride. "We believe having the unique perspective of four trainers gives our submissives the highest chance of success outside these walls."

"That makes a lot of sense," Thane says, nodding his approval.

"But you don't think it's overkill?" I ask, pressing the man for the fun of it.

"Not at all. We want our students to experience as much as possible during the six-week course and having a panel of four allows us to do that effectively."

I like that Mr. Gallant answers each question with thoughtful consideration. I can see why he has been given such an important position in the school.

Thane is obviously fascinated by what the man has shared. "You mentioned practicums. Does that mean the trainers scene with each submissive?"

"The course is customized for the individual student,

and the most qualified trainer or trainers are chosen for each particular lesson based on their skill and experience in that area."

"I've heard that submissives who graduate from your school are highly sought after and are some of the best-trained in the world," Anderson states.

"They are, and do you want to know why?" Gallant asks.

He has my attention now.

"People mistakenly think we train our students to meet the needs of a variety of Dominants, but that's not what we do here. We allow our students to explore their BDSM tendencies in the safety of this controlled environment, while correcting and critiquing them. It makes for a submissive who is confident in their skill and knows where their true passions lie."

Thane rubs his chin, smiling. "My mind is blown. This school is everything I'd hoped it would be and more."

Mr. Gallant nods, glancing briefly at his watch. "Our students are about to arrive, so I must ask you to take your places."

We walk back to the area and watch staff members scurry about as they finish setting up for the auction. Not long after, the vetted Doms and Dommes arrive. Most of them gather in groups, speaking quietly amongst themselves. It seems they know each other, but I notice a few stand back, choosing not to interact with the others as they wait for the auction to begin.

If having observers attend were unusual, one wouldn't know it. Not one person glances in our direction, leaving us plenty of time to stand quietly contemplating our own thoughts.

And the only thing I can think about is Marquis Gray's question.

Why am I here?

I'm here because Thane invited me. I'm here because it sounded interesting and I didn't want to be left out.

My mind starts drifting to more general thoughts…

I'm here because I needed to distance myself from what happened to Tatianna. I'm here because my father is a dick and my brothers are strangers. I'm here because I wanted to forge a new path where I am in control. I'm here to escape my past.

But, even that line of thinking feels as though it's lacking, and I return to the original question.

Why am I here?

I'm here because God put me on this Earth. I'm here because I'm a fighter who doesn't back down. I've never backed down, even as a young child. I'm here because the world needs someone like me.

Such a simple question, but one that invites a multitude of answers.

I stand a little taller and scan the room, feeling a part of the experience even though I am only a silent observer here.

All eyes turn to the stage when a man walks out and moves to the mic stand on the left side of the stage near us. He says nothing but nods in acknowledgement toward those gathered.

Four people, including Marquis Gray, walk out and sit behind a table on the right side of the stage.

I hear quiet voices behind the partition and then silence.

"We begin today's auction with Miss Jackson."

A young woman walks out onto the stage dressed in a tight corset, short mini skirt, and stilettos that accentuate her sexy legs. She stands confidently in the center of the stage with her head tilted slightly upward while her gaze remains on the floor.

"Miss Jackson is twenty-three and is an elementary teacher outside these walls. Her trainers describe her as an active learner. Her fantasy involves the naughty schoolgirl scenario. There are no additional changes to the sexual fantasy. I will start the bidding at seventy-five."

The auctioneer starts rapidly rattling off numbers as the bids steadily climb to three hundred. "Going once…going twice…sold to Master Rogers for three hundred dollars."

One of the loners in the crowd moves up and collects the submissive from the stage. He guides her to where he was originally standing and they wait silently for the next auction, his arm wrapped possessively around her waist.

I can feel the girl's palpable excitement even from where I'm standing.

Two strangers about to scene together outside the walls of this institution must be a heady experience. No wonder the vetting process is so complicated here. Allowing a student to leave in the hands of a stranger could lead to abuse in the wrong hands.

"Next, we have Ms. Adams."

The submissive who walks out is a tall brunette. She oozes sexuality, and I can already hear low murmurs from the crowd.

"Ms. Adams is twenty-six, and a corporate lawyer outside these walls. Her trainers describe her as intelligent and open to extreme stimulation. Her fantasy involves the stripper/prostitute scenario. There are no additional changes to her sexual fantasy. I will start the bidding at seventy-five."

In no time at all, the bidding jumps up to four hundred and fifty. The lucky winner walks up to the submissive with a confident smile, clearly pleased with his purchase.

She takes the arm he offers, and he guides her off the stage as he smirks at the other Doms.

The auctioneer states, "Our next submissive is Miss Reed."

A petite woman walks onto the stage wearing the same attire as the other two women. Despite her small stature, she walks with catlike grace in those tall stilettos.

"Miss Reed is thirty-two and is a hotel manager outside these walls. Her trainers describe her as eager and obedient. Her fantasy involves double penetration. There is one change to her sexual fantasy. She requests that the two men pretend to be brothers."

There are low chuckles among the crowd.

As before, the auctioneer starts the bidding at seventy-five.

The bids come in slowly at first, but it's quickly apparent that a pair of Doms are determined to win her. After a healthy back and forth with another set of

Dominants, the two get the winning bid at five hundred.

They both walk up to the stage and take turns kissing her before escorting her off the platform.

"Our next submissive is Miss Sanchez."

A curvy vixen with long, wavy dark hair walks out onto the stage.

"Miss Sanchez is twenty-eight and is a stockbroker outside these walls. Her trainers describe her as assertive but pliable. Her fantasy involves sex in a public place. There are no additional changes to her sexual fantasy. I will start the bidding at seventy-five."

The Domme who ends up winning the bid walks up to her and caresses the submissive seductively as we all watch.

I hear a soft moan escape from the submissive's lips.

Already the Domme is delivering on the fantasy— and they haven't even left the stage yet.

Once she's escorted off, the auctioneer states, "This concludes today's auction. A simple reminder for the winners. Once you have purchased a sub, you are not allowed to bid on her again for the remainder of the training."

I'm surprised there are so few submissives. I glance at the four trainers who are talking amongst themselves as the crowd begins filing out of the commons. They get up and disappear behind the partition.

Turning to Thane, I ask hoping he will know the answer. "Why so few?"

"Marquis Gray explained that their courses are small because of how customized the classes are."

I nod. "That would explain why the submissives are

so highly sought after. There are only a few to choose from."

Anderson folds his arms. "Hell, I would have enjoyed being part of the bidding."

"I agree," I tell him, thinking back on the tall brunette. "I definitely wouldn't have minded a lap dance from the lawyer."

Anderson slaps me on the back, chuckling as we start walking toward the elevator after the commons finally clears out.

Why am I here?

The question hits me again when I spot Gallant speaking with one of the staff members. It seems providence because I'm now certain I have an answer. "I'll meet you two upstairs. There's something I need to do."

"Don't you go looking for trouble," Anderson jokes.

Thane gives me a questioning look, but steps into the elevator along with Anderson. Once the doors close, I walk over to Gallant to find he's still in the middle of a conversation.

When he glances over at me, he quickly excuses himself and asks, "What is it, Mr. Durov?"

Suddenly feeling awkward, I mumble, "I wanted to mention that Thane Davis is an excellent teacher."

He smiles kindly. "I suspected as much by the questions he's peppered me with."

Seeing he understands, I tell him, "Thane isn't someone to mention it, but he's looking to expand his teaching efforts in the area of BDSM once he graduates from college. I could see him being an ideal fit for the

Center."

"He'd need to gain considerable experience and credentials to be considered for a position as trainer at our Center," Mr. Gallant explains.

"I was told that the school started up a Dominant Training course."

He raises an eyebrow. "We have. Curious that Marquis Gray would mention it to you."

"He didn't tell me directly, but he did mention it to Thane, and Marquis Gray doesn't seem the type of person to engage in idle conversation with a person."

Gallant chuckles. "No, he does not."

He glances at the staff member, who is patiently waiting, so I quickly end our conversation. "Before I leave, I wanted you to know how highly regarded Thane Davis is at college, as well as our BDSM community at the dungeon."

"I'll certainly speak to Marquis Gray about what you've shared."

I offer my hand to him. "It's been a pleasure meeting you, Mr. Gallant."

"Likewise, Rytsar Durov."

I stride toward the elevators feeling good that Marquis Gray's question motivated me to act. Looking around the commons, I could absolutely see Thane working here in the future.

I find my friends waiting for me upstairs near the reception desk.

"Get everything squared away in the bathroom?" Anderson asks.

I laugh. "Why don't you go downstairs and find out."

"Cleared the whole commons, did you?"

Thane shakes his head, smiling to himself. "I don't know about you two, but the auction has left me needing to play with a sub."

"Couldn't agree more," Anderson replies, adjusting his jeans. "I'm in *serious* need."

"*Da!*" I glance down at his straining jeans. "You look like you are about to burst out with need."

I follow closely behind Anderson, snickering, as he walks stiffly toward the exit. Before we make it outside, Marquis Gray appears out of nowhere like some kind of specter.

"Thank you for coming, gentlemen. I trust you found the auction informative—as well as stimulating."

"That's an understatement," Anderson jokes.

When Marquis Gray meets his gaze, Anderson puts all kidding aside, stating in a solemn voice, "I'm curious how the scenarios will play out for each sub."

"As are we, which is why the students will return here after their respective scenes so we can debrief with them."

Thane's eyes widen with understanding and I can see the wheels in his head turning. "That's brilliant. There would be a wealth of information a submissive could gain by discussing the encounter with four experienced Doms."

Marquis Gray nods thoughtfully. "Our intent with every scene our subs experience is to help them grow in confidence and skill while they navigate their strengths and weaknesses. It's the reason I wouldn't train anywhere else."

"I can certainly understand why," Thane states with admiration.

The trainer hands us each his business card with the Center's information. "I expect a call later detailing your thoughts about the auction."

The look in Thane's eyes as he takes the card from Marquis Gray leaves no doubt that my brother has found his true calling.

It brings me great satisfaction to witness Thane take this first step toward his destiny.

Snapping Point

I shoot up out of my bed from a dead sleep, screaming her name. "Tatianna!"

The loss of her hits me full in the chest and I struggle to breathe. I close my eyes, but the tears still come, knowing I will never see her again.

A sob escapes my lips as I lie back down and relive the reoccurring nightmare that has haunted me ever since that day she was kidnapped. The dream always begins with me looking in the mirror as I adjust my black tie in preparation for Tatianna's eighteenth birthday.

Titov bangs on the door. I forget the damn tie as I rush to open it, spurred on by the desperate sound in his voice.

"He took Tatianna!" Titov screams.

A chill grips my heart knowing she is in danger. "*Who* took her?"

I need to know whom I must kill.

"Yuri. He kidnapped her to pay his gambling debt."

"What?" I roar, fighting the urge to punch Titov in

the face for putting his sister in danger. I've told him repeatedly not to hang around such *bratva* lowlife.

But there's no time to waste! We must find her as soon as possible.

I grab my keys and rush out the door. We have a hard time hunting Yuri down, but when we finally locate him, Tatianna is nowhere to be found.

The motherfucker refuses to tell me where she is, so I go apeshit and beat it out of him.

In my dream, just like in real life, my blood runs cold the moment he informs me that Tatianna has been sold to a slaver. With my hands wrapped around his neck, I force him to tell us exactly where she's been taken.

I nearly choke him to death before he finally spills the location. I look at Titov and ask, "Can I kill him now?"

"Don't," he insists. "We may need him later."

Snarling, I choke him until he passes out and hogtie him. Even in my dreams, I don't get the satisfaction of killing Yuri.

It didn't take us long to drive to the location where she was being held in real life—but in my nightmare when I start driving, my eyes close against my will and I am unable to see. I can't open them and am forced to drive blind. I fear that at any second we will die in a fiery crash.

Still, I press down on the gas pedal knowing Tatianna's life depends on it.

Relief floods through my body when Titov informs me that we've arrived at the location. Like magic, my eyes open and I can see again.

I have yet to understand the reason for the blindness in my dream, but the terror and anxiety it produces is real and haunts me hours after the dream is over.

The nightmare continues as the two of us race from the car to start up a long flight of stairs on the outside of the building. Precious minutes tick by, but the damn stairs never end.

The reality is that I never caught up to Tatianna, because the slaver left with her just minutes before we arrived—but, in my nightmare, we finally reach the top of the stairs and come to a red door. I don't hesitate and open it.

I see the slaver dragging her away. Tatianna turns to me, completely terrified, and cries, "Save me, Anton!"

When I start running toward her, my feet sink into the floor like it is made of quicksand and I can't move. All I can do is cry out her name while she is dragged away kicking and screaming.

That's when I wake up—every single fucking time.

Seeing her in the hands of the slaver, knowing what he will do to her but being powerless to stop it is horrifying on so many levels.

At least in the nightmare, Tatianna sees Titov and I before she disappears…

Tears roll down my face as I lie in bed, knowing what really happened. Tatianna never knew we were minutes away from saving her.

No. She was ripped away from her family, abused by slavers, and left alone in that horrific reality—never knowing how tragically close she'd come to being rescued from all of it.

Tatianna lived that ungodly hell for five months before we finally found her. But, by then, she was just skin and bones—a shell of herself.

I live with the heavy guilt of having failed her every day of my life.

If I could, I would have died to save her that day.

Even though we eventually rescued Tatianna, we lost her to suicide a few months later.

She was my *one*. My soulmate, and the future mother of my children. When Yuri kidnapped her, he not only stole her future, but mine as well—and that of generations to come.

Tatianna should have only known kindness and love. The cruelty of what happened to her burns like a raging fire inside of me.

I throw off my covers and jump out of bed, needing to redirect this anger before it consumes me where I stand.

Picking up hand weights, I start pumping my arms, trying not to think about what she suffered under the hands of the slavers, but the images won't stop, and I feel the need to hurt something.

I get dressed and head out of the room to jog in the darkness of predawn.

My scalp begins to prickle when I realize that I'm being followed. I run a little faster to confirm it. When I hear the footsteps behind me pick up their pace, I smile to myself.

If this is a minion of Thane's mother, this will be fun!

Turing around, I stare out into the darkness and roar out my challenge. "You want a piece of Rytsar Durov?"

I raise my fists, ready to annihilate the threat.

Unfortunately, the coward turns and runs. I growl in frustration when I hear his footsteps quickly receding in the darkness.

My body is in full fight mode now, but I have no release. Swallowing down the rage, I start running again.

I feel dangerous, as if the slightest thing will cause me to snap.

Later that same day, Anderson invites Thane and me to a kegger with his other friends. Although I don't enjoy the taste of beer, I need to be around good people, so I agree to join them there.

Before I go, however, I visit the dungeon. I haven't come to scene, only to observe.

In my current state, I'm far too wound up to release that kind of negative energy on a submissive. Instead, I stand back and watch while other Doms put their subs through their paces.

I take pleasure watching the expression on a sub's face as the pain transitions into pleasure and she begins to fly, her eyes fluttering when she begins to enter subspace.

Watching their pleasure helps ease my soul.

After spending several hours at the dungeon, I finally feel prepared to face a house full of strangers as I party with my friends.

Unfortunately, I can find neither Thane nor Anderson when I arrive.

I search the multitude of rooms in the large frat house but come up short, so I decide to head out to the backyard. My anxiety increases as I bump against people crowded into the kitchen.

Gritting my teeth, I force my way out the back door.

There I find a group having a drunken pool party. A frat boy jumps into the pool, still holding his plastic cup of beer, to the applause of his drunk friends—but there's no sign of Thane or Anderson.

My anxiety rises to an alarming level, and it feels as if I'd never visited the dungeon tonight.

I prepare to leave when I hear Anderson's voice just around the corner of the house. I head there, needing his calming influence.

Rounding the corner, I bump into Samantha.

I glower at her, the pain and humiliation of that night returning in full as I stare at her. I suddenly can't breathe as images of Tatianna flood my mind, and it all mixes into a terrible ball of fire in my gut.

Samantha stumbles backward in shock. "I'm sorry, Ryt—" She cuts herself off before daring to say my name and sputters nervously, "I…didn't see you."

I glare at her, but I don't see Samantha anymore. I see all the maggots who hurt my Tatianna, and roar with rage.

My vision fades to red as I suddenly release the intense pressure that has been building into a merciless storm of vengeance.

I'm not aware that my hands are wrapped around her neck until I hear Thane's far-off voice.

"Durov, stop! You're killing her!"

It doesn't seem real until he yells loudly in my ear, "Anton! Let go!"

Aware of my surroundings again, I'm shocked to find myself straddling Samantha, who lies underneath me on the ground. Both of my hands are wrapped around her neck.

Her eyes are open, but she looks up at me with a glassy stare.

I feel Thane pull at my arms but I'm frozen and can't move.

Anderson joins in and, between the two of them, they are able to pry my hands from her throat.

I stare at Samantha with remorse, certain that I've killed her.

Thankfully, her body begins to spasm as she gasps for air and starts blinking her eyes, struggling to take in a deep breath.

Thane grabs my arm. "We have to get out of here— now."

But I am rooted to where I stand, shocked by the knowledge that she would be dead right now if Thane hadn't intervened.

Anderson has to physically push me toward the backyard gate. "Go with Thane. I'll take care of her."

As I'm guided out, I turn back once to see Anderson helping Samantha sit up.

I take solace in the fact that she seems okay.

However, I'm not.

"What the hell happened back there?" Thane demands, turning around to face me on our way back to the campus.

My voice is hollow when I answer. "I don't know. I've been carrying around this rage toward Tatianna's abusers, and when I saw Samantha tonight, all the raw feelings came rushing back—"

Thane closes his eyes, his voice unsteady when he says, "You almost killed her."

I look down at my hands, horrified. "All I saw was red. I wasn't aware of anything until I heard you calling my name."

When Thane opens his eyes and meets my gaze, they are filled with concern—and guilt. "I had no idea she was going to be there and warned her to leave as soon as I saw her. She was on her way out when you…"

I shudder, clenching my hands into fists. "I didn't intend to hurt her."

"I had no idea things were this bad for you." He places his hand on my shoulder. "I'm sorry I've been so blind."

I shake my head, unsettled by my loss of control. "I can't be trusted."

Thane responds with compassion. "You need therapy. This isn't something you fix with time—not after all you've been through."

"You're right, brother. I will turn myself in to the police, even though this will crush my poor mother."

"Don't," Thane states firmly.

I frown at him. "It was attempted murder, whether I intended to kill her or not. Everyone saw it."

When I see tears come to his eyes, it guts me. "Wait."

"For what?" I snarl. "I refuse to be dragged away in handcuffs."

"Let me talk to Samantha before you go to the police."

I already know my fate and sigh. Thane will never forgive himself for this. "You have been a good friend."

"No, you are not doing that to me," he growls angrily, baring the scar on his wrist. "We made a promise to each other."

"I know," I chuckle humorlessly. "I don't plan to leave this planet because of that vow. But I do not think I will see you for a very long time."

His eyes flash with pain.

"You must rehabilitate her." I put my hand on the back of his neck and press my forehead against his. "You must do it for both of us, brother. Go back to Samantha. Make sure she is okay."

"What about you?"

I sigh, rubbing my bald head in agitation. "I need some time alone, comrade."

"Are you sure?"

"*Da.*"

I see the agony in his eyes. His soul is torn between his concern for Samantha and his loyalty to me.

"I will be fine," I assure him. "I just need a long walk to clear my head."

I can tell he is hesitant to leave me alone, so I turn and call out as I walk away, "I'll be fine!"

I wander the streets aimlessly, unsure what my future holds after tonight. I eventually find myself next to a large city park. As I walk down the jogging path, it's not long before that prickling sensation returns, alerting me to the fact the stalker has returned.

Refusing to play the victim, I slow down and listen. As soon as I pinpoint the direction he's coming from, I turn around abruptly and roar like a raging lion, running straight toward him in the dark.

The guy screams like a terrified girl as he bolts. Determined to catch him, I run blind. The closer I get, the more he gasps for air. It's obvious the man is out of shape.

But just as I am about to tackle him, my foot slams into a rock and I crash to the ground, the breath knocked clean out of me.

His gasps grow fainter while I struggle back onto my feet. A sharp pain shoots through my right ankle when I try to put weight on it.

"*Gavno!*" I cry out in frustration, knowing there's no hope of catching the bastard now.

I start hobbling around, desperate to find a place to sit down.

I'm relieved when I see a lone bench lit up by the streetlight above it but, as I get closer, I see that there's a guy curled up on it, sleeping. In no mood to walk any farther, I clear my throat to wake him.

The moment he stirs, I ask, "Mind if I sit here?"

He rolls over to face me and immediate sits up, making room. It throws me off when he puts his hands together and bows his head slightly. I look the kid over, realizing by his features that he must be of Japanese descent.

Grunting in pain, I sit down on the bench and bend

down to massage my throbbing ankle.

"What happened?" he asks quietly.

I glance at the kid who appears to be a few years younger than I am. Not in the mood for conversation, I state simply, "Twisted my ankle and just needed to get off it for a few minutes."

"Take as much time as you need."

We sit there in silence for several minutes before I hear his stomach growl. He pretends not to notice, keeping his serene expression.

The fact that the guy is sleeping on a park bench makes it safe to assume he hasn't eaten for a while. Not one to watch people suffer—unless it's for my pleasure—I pull out my wallet and take out my cash, handing him a thick wad of bills.

He shakes his head. "I can't accept charity. I work for my money."

"What do you do?" I ask, respecting his pride.

The kid shrugs. "I doubt you've heard of it."

"Try me," I insist, leaving the bills on the bench while I go back to massaging my ankle.

"Are you familiar with Kinbaku?"

I nod. "Yeah, it's the Japanese style of bondage."

He smiles, looking genuinely pleased that I know that.

I smirk, gesturing to the park bench. "It doesn't look like it pays very well."

Chuckling, he sweeps his long bangs back. "I've just moved here from Japan and haven't found employment yet."

"All the more reason to take my cash," I tell him,

pushing it toward him.

His smile grows wider. "Your generosity is appreciated, but she needs it more than I do." The kid points to an old woman sleeping on the ground, covered in a ratty blanket, her arms wrapped tightly around a shopping cart that must hold all her worldly possessions.

"Fine." I get up, purposely not favoring my injured ankle in order to test it. Walking over to her, I quietly stash the wad of cash in a plastic bag in the center of the shopping cart, then return to the bench and sit down.

I hand the kid a twenty that I've kept for him. "As a fellow Dom, at least let me buy you a meal."

He raises his eyebrows in surprise and holds out his hand to shake mine. "It is a pleasure to meet another Master."

"I'm Rytsar Durov. And you are?"

"Ren Nosaka."

I shake his hand firmly, pressing the cash into his palm. "Get yourself a decent meal, Ren Nosaka."

He stares down at the twenty in his hand, clearly feeling uneasy about taking it.

"Seems as if fate orchestrated this impromptu meeting," I tell him, thinking back on Marquis Gray's question.

"Why do you say that?"

Pulling out my wallet again, I find the business card I'd slipped in there after my visit to the Center and hand it to him. "You should give this place a call. I'm positive they'll have a need for your unique talent."

The kid reads the card aloud and smiles. "The Submissive Training Center…" He looks at me gratefully and bows his head again. "Thank you."

I glance at the cash in his hand. "Next time, you can take me out for lunch."

He meets my gaze, promising solemnly, "It would be my honor, Rytsar Durov."

The kid continues to stare into my eyes.

Feeling uncomfortably exposed under his penetrating gaze, I look away as I stand up. "I need to head out."

As I walk away, he calls out behind me, "You *are* strong enough for whatever comes next. Just remember to breathe."

A chill runs down my spine. I'm surprised by the effect his words have on me. Rather than turn around and question him, I take it as a sign.

I know exactly what I need to do now.

Mamulya

I hate leaving my brother behind. It feels as if I am physically ripping a limb off from my body.

But I have no choice. I can't be trusted around Samantha.

I would be in jail right now for murder if Thane hadn't intervened. It is a terrible and sobering reality.

Although I will never forgive Samantha for what she's done, she does not deserve to die. I cared for her…once. I've seen that vulnerable side of her, and I know her strengths. The world would be less without her in it.

So, I must leave.

Samantha cares deeply for Thane and has proven that on multiple occasions when he was threatened. He may need her protection in the future when I'm not around, and Samantha is no coward.

While my heart still rages, I take comfort in knowing that Samantha will never have that kind of power over me again.

No woman will.

So, I'm forced to return to Russia whether I am ready or not.

The time has come to reconnect with my motherland—and my past.

Thane and Anderson come to see me off. I knew that it would be hard on Thane, but I'm surprised to see that the cattleman looks distraught as well.

"Why the long face?" I tease, pinching Anderson's cheek as if he's a chubby baby.

He automatically smacks my hands away, grinning as he rubs his cheek. "What can I say? I'm going to miss your irritating presence."

I chuckle, but with little humor behind it—I don't want to leave.

Anderson frowns. "I was looking forward to us graduating together, since Thane is still set on graduating early. And I had the best prank planned for you…"

"I wish I could be here to enjoy it."

"Me, too, Russki. Me, too."

Anderson nods to Thane. "I'll head out so you can say your goodbyes. Meet me at the diner so we can cry over coffee and cinnamon rolls about the horny Russian who got away."

Anderson gives me one last parting sock in the shoulder before walking away.

It feels so final that I call out, "We're still on with

our mothers' cooking showdown. Right, cattleman?"

He turns back and tips an imaginary hat. "Wouldn't miss it for the world, Durov. But don't hate me when my mama wins."

I snort. "Right…"

There is a look of sadness on his face just before he turns away. If Anderson is this distressed about my departure, I can only imagine how Thane feels.

However, my comrade hides it by distancing himself emotionally. I understand and am not offended—but I am sad for us both.

I'm being forced to face a future without Thane by my side and it leaves me off balance.

It's unnerving that I've become a student who no longer has an appetite for learning, and a man of passion who now lacks direction and purpose.

Facing an unknown tomorrow is daunting.

"Goodbye, brother," I tell Thane, my voice catching slightly as I hold out my hand to him.

"I wish you didn't have to leave," he states, shaking my hand firmly.

"It's the only way. We both know it."

Thane nods curtly. "Call me once you settle in. I plan to head to Russia for a visit after I graduate. You can give me a proper introduction to your homeland then."

I put my hand on his shoulder. "I admire that about you, comrade. Despite everything that's happened, you've still maintained your goal of graduating a year ahead of us. Such a momentous accomplishment should be celebrated, and I will throw you a *grand* party in Russia, the likes of which you have never known."

He smiles self-consciously. "I haven't graduated yet."

I know he will and regret that I won't be here when he walks across the stage to receive his diploma. "I wish I could be there to cheer you on, *moy droog.*"

Guilt flits across his eyes but he claps me on the back. "I promise Russia will be my first stop after graduation."

Leaning in, I whisper, "I do not blame you, brother."

He sighs, my words undoing his carefully constructed emotional barrier. He stares at me sadly, admitting, "I've questioned my actions ever since that night. If I hadn't insisted on teaching Samantha about the BDSM lifestyle…if I hadn't introduced her to you…if I hadn't left—"

"There is no point in questioning the past. Trust me. I've driven myself insane doing the same thing after I lost Tatianna." I unconsciously clutch at my heart. The pain of narrowly missing her still claws at me. A matter of a few minutes, and I could have saved her—and me.

"No," I assure him, "the only thing either of us can do is move forward from here. We learn from the past, *da*, but it benefits no one to drown in it."

Thane looks deeply into my eyes. "All the tragedy you've survived makes you truly unique. You are a man who will do great things, Anton. I fully believe that."

I shrug off such a heavy burden. "I need a few years of stupidity and fun before I try to make something of myself."

Thane nods. "You've certainly earned that right."

"But I know you," I state. "You plan to forge your future right out of college, don't you?"

"I don't have a choice, really. I have to do whatever it takes to ensure financial independence from the Beast." Looking off into the distance, a slight smile curls Thane's lips. "But I know there will come a day when she'll come for my money—and I can't wait to see the look on her face when I tell her where to go."

I grin, imagining the moment myself. "That will be a good day, brother."

"May you find closure after the many wrongs you have suffered."

I punch my fist into my palm, grinding it. "I only know of one way to bring about the kind of closure I need."

Thane suddenly looks concerned. "You have been gifted with intelligence. Don't lower yourself to their level in the pursuit of revenge."

"Don't worry, comrade. I will strive to be creative in my extracurricular endeavors," I assure him with a smirk.

Thane looks away with a pained expression, muttering, "Strange. I already miss you and you haven't even left yet."

Feeling exactly the same, I reach out and give the man a hug.

"We are never far away from each other, *moy droog*," I remind him, holding up my wrist to show him my scar. "We are forever connected, you and I."

Thane stares down at his own wrist and says nothing for a moment. I wonder what he's thinking but, before I can ask, he holds his hand out to me with a forced smile. "Until we meet in Russia."

"Until then, brother," I answer, shaking his hand.

I turn to go, ignoring the sense of foreboding I have in the pit of my stomach.

I don't want to leave him or this place…

I retreat into myself, once I'm on the plane bound for Russia, remembering the first time my father strapped me to the pole and rained his hatred down on me—proclaiming me the family's whipping boy.

Although I grew up aware of his sadistic tendencies, I never anticipated he would inflict them on his own son. As a mere boy of five, I was not prepared the day I received that first punishment from his terrifying whip.

While I may have cried under the ferocity of his many beatings, I never gave my father the satisfaction of conquering my spirit. I had no control over his whip, so I had to endure his punishments, but I never allowed him to touch my soul.

Looking out at the huge clouds in the distance, I shift in my seat, overcome by that unsettling feeling again.

I suspect it has everything to do with Tatianna and my reluctance to accept that she is no longer a part of this world—or my future.

I hope seeing my mother will stave off the heartache I feel in returning to Russia. Perhaps this time I will find relief from the pain that haunts me.

Hell, I still hold out hope I may find additional strength in connecting with my four brothers, now that we've had time apart. I won't allow the barrier my father set between us to continue to rule over our lives.

There's no doubt that returning home under these circumstances makes this the bravest thing I've ever done.

Still, I am determined to make a future for myself.

I pull out a notebook and begin sketching a picture of my mother. She is the only constant left in my life.

I begin outlining her face, filling in her delicate features—those elegantly arched eyebrows and big eyes that shine with love. I sketch her delicate nose next, followed by her high cheekbones. I smile as I draw her lips. Mamulya is always smiling—except for those times when my father makes her cry.

I snarl under my breath, refusing to let my father taint this portrait of her. I continue, trying to capture the fine wisps of hair that frame her face. When I'm done, I stare down at it, my heart feeling lighter.

It is good I am headed home. I have missed her.

Although I haven't told anyone I am returning, I'm surprised to find no one at the family estate. Talking to the staff, I'm distressed to learn my mother is no longer living here with my father.

My protective instincts kick in as I head to the family manor just outside of Moscow, where I've been told she is staying.

What has my father done this time? Why was I not informed?

Hitting the gas, I speed down the streets, not caring if I get pulled over. Once I arrive, I pound on the door, holding my breath, hoping against hope she is okay.

I stand back when I hear the lock slide, and then wait

with bated breath as the door slowly opens.

The expression of pure joy I see on my mother's face is something I will never forget. One second we are staring at each other, and the next I feel my mother's arms wrap around me. "Oh, Anton!"

There is magic in her touch and I close my eyes, savoring the purity of her love. It's as if I'm a child again, safe in my mother's arms.

She finally breaks our embrace so she can stand back and look at me.

"What a wonderful surprise," she gushes. "You're the last person I expected when I opened the door."

I wipe a grateful tear from my eye on seeing that she is well. "I wanted to surprise you, *Mamulya.*"

She laughs. Oh, how that laughter soothes my soul. "Well, you certainly did that." She takes a hold of my hand. "Come in and tell me everything!"

I sit down next to her on the antique couch upholstered in a tapestry passed down in our family for generations. Everything in this house is a part of the Durov legacy, but the only thing that makes it feel like home is the woman in front of me.

"So, tell me. How long are you here for?"

I smile, trying to hide my warring emotions. "I'm home for good."

She tilts her head, her sweet lips turning downward. "What about your degree? Don't you still have another year left after this one?"

I hate for her to worry, so I chuckle lightly when I answer. "Simply put, college wasn't challenging enough."

She pats my hand, her eyes shining with pride. "You

always were the smartest person I've ever known."

I lean toward her and smile. "Only because I take after you."

Hearing her trill of laughter lightens my heart. "Oh, Anton, you're such a flatterer."

I'm speaking the truth, even if she refuses to accept it. My mother is the only reason this family remains intact. Without her thoughtful influence, I swear my father would have died years ago by his own arrogance and stupidity.

"So, tell me about your friends Thane, Brad and Samantha."

I don't know how I do it, but I manage to keep my smile at the mention of Samantha's name. I don't ever want *Mamulya* to know what happened between us.

I laugh again. "Let's just say that my friends hate losing their favorite Russian, but they're all doing well enough. Thane still plans to graduate this year. As for the other two, they'll have to learn to struggle on without me." To change the subject, I inform her, "Anderson has challenged you to a cook-off with his mother."

She claps her hands in delight. "Wouldn't that be fun?"

I love that about her. Even though my mother is a far better cook, I know she will make certain Anderson's mother feels welcomed and cherished simply because Anderson is my friend. I appreciate that anyone I care about instantly becomes family to her.

That's so opposite of my father.

"Where will this challenge be held?" she asks me.

"In Russia. You will have the hometown advantage."

Her smile grows wider. "I can't wait to meet your American friends."

"It won't be for a while. However, Thane promises to visit as soon as he graduates. I can't wait for you to meet him, *Mamulya*."

She lays her hand on my cheek and looks into my eyes. "It must have been hard for you to leave them behind."

My mother's gaze can be dangerous because she is incredibly perceptive. So, I lean in and give her a quick kiss on the forehead. "I can't run away forever from what happened to Tatianna, but I am glad you pushed me to leave when you did. I needed time to find a new path."

She looks at me with compassion. "What path did you find?"

I laugh uncomfortably, pulling away from her. "I'll let you know when I figure that out."

"Anton," she says, her voice quiet but somber. "What's the real reason you came back?"

I hold my breath, not wanting to say a word.

Smiling sadly, she asks, "Did your father fail to pay your tuition? I've been worried about that."

I let my breath out slowly, grateful that I am still able to keep my secret. "What's going on with him? Father cut the rental on the beach house, but I figured he was just trying to assert his fatherly authority over me."

My mother looks at me with concern and states hesitantly, "Your father has amassed a great deal of debt."

"How? Our family has never lacked for money."

She stares down at her hands, looking distraught.

"He's gambled it all away, Anton. It's become a sickness he can't control." She sighs sadly. "I thought leaving would be enough to shake him out of it, but it's only gotten worse since I moved out."

"Why didn't you tell me?"

Her smile is full of love when she answers, "You've had enough to deal with."

"What about my brothers? Have they done nothing to stop this?"

"Your father associates with the Koslovs now. I don't want any of my boys getting involved."

"He is consorting with the *bratva*?" I cry out in anger. "Has he gone completely insane?"

"Maybe he has," she whispers, tears forming in her eyes.

I can't handle my mother crying and immediately hold her. "It'll be okay. I will handle this."

She pulls away, gently cupping my cheek. "I don't want you getting involved either, Anton. They are a dangerous family to cross."

I squeeze her small frame tightly.

I will figure something out. There's no way I will allow my father to gamble away the Durov legacy.

How I wish my father could be the kind of man my mother deserves. In every way, he has failed her.

I snarl angrily, "I despise that man. I wish you'd never crossed paths with him."

"No! Don't ever say that," she protests. "If we hadn't married, I would never have had you."

"I am not worth your suffering, *Mamulya*."

She laughs. "You act as if it's always been bad, but

your father and I were in love once." She touches my chest and smiles. "You were born out of that love, Anton."

I draw her to me again, holding her tight.

I need to forget the world momentarily and concentrate on reuniting with her. I have missed my mother more than I realized.

"What do you say if we made *piroshkis* together?" she asks.

My stomach growls in answer. "It has been far too long since I've eaten one of your *piroshki*."

I've always loved watching my mother cook. It was something only she and I shared.

It was our conversations in the kitchen while I was growing up that helped form me into the man I've become.

Following her into the kitchen, I start getting out all the ingredients she will need for the bread.

"What kind would you like today, savory or sweet?" she asks.

"Savory."

My mouth starts watering at the thought of the meaty roll as I go to the refrigerator to get out the ground beef, egg, and onion for the filling while she starts making the bread.

As she works, my mother reminisces about her courtship with my father. Although it is hard for me to hear, knowing what he has become, it does help me understand how she has remained loyal to him all these years.

"Your father was as handsome as you are," she begins, smiling lovingly at me. "Tall and robust, with devilish blue eyes I couldn't resist."

She laughs as she begins kneading the dough. "My mother warned me not to get involved with him."

I frown. "She was right."

"Ah, but young love will not be denied," she replies, her eyes sparkling with old memories. "Even when my parents forbade me to date him, I would still sneak out at night whenever Vladimir came to pick me up."

I shake my head. Even with the knowledge I would not be alive if he hadn't pursued her, I still wish my mother hadn't fallen in love with the man.

I offer to brown the ground beef, stabbing at it to take out my aggression as I break up the meat.

She continues, lulling me with her light, pleasant voice. "I'd led such a sheltered life, but your father showed me that there was a whole new world I never knew existed."

I feel sick, thinking what it must have been like for her the first time he introduced her to his sadism. "Were you terrified when you realized what he truly was?"

She smiles, blushing slightly. "Oh, no. If you believe that, you are very mistaken."

"How was it, then?"

I know this is getting into uncomfortable territory considering she's my mother, but I need to hear it.

She stops kneading and asks, "Do you really want to know?"

"*Da.*"

Her blush deepens. "When Vladimir took me to the secret dungeon, I won't lie, I was excited. It wasn't until then that I realized there were other people who craved pain as I did. The night your father introduced me to how sexy he could make pain be, my life completely changed."

"So, you truly enjoyed it?" I ask her, having always assumed she'd been dragged into his sadism against her will.

She nods, looking at me coyly. "But my parents would never have understood."

"*Nyet*," I agree, looking down at the pot as I stir the meat and onions together.

"I was so proud when you chose to pursue the same path as your father."

I put down the spoon to face her. "Why?"

She smiles at the question. "Because I knew how happy you would make other women. It is a gift, Anton. And, based on what your father told me, you are even more talented than he is."

I frown, surprised to hear it. "Father always finds fault in everything I do."

She looks at me with sympathy.

I don't want to spoil this moment talking about him, so I tell her, "It is good to know you were a natural masochist."

"Maybe now you can understand why I fell so hard for him. He not only accepted me for who I was, he let me bask in it."

It is hard for me to imagine my father as anything but the tyrant he is now.

She finishes kneading the dough and covers it to rest. "Even though things have turned out the way they have,

I have no doubt he and I were destined for each other. Seeing you here now, I am even more convinced."

I set the meat aside to cool, while she starts the water for the hard-boiled eggs.

"You deserved better," I mutter.

She comes up to me, her hands covered in flour, and tweaks my nose. "You are the best thing that has ever happened to me. You, and your brothers."

I growl under my breath.

"Anton, I know your father made it difficult to be close to them, but don't give up on your brothers. There will come a day when the five of you will need each other's strength."

I huff in disbelief. "They've never cared about me."

She caresses my cheek. "You're wrong, son. Now that they are grown and out from under your father's influence, they will connect with you."

I shake my head bitterly. "I doubt it. The only brother I have is Thane Davis."

She reaches out and lightly rubs the scar on my wrist. "I wondered what this was about."

I stare down at the scar. "He saved my sanity."

She looks deep into my eyes. "Which is all the more reason why I must meet him. I would like to have a heart-to-heart with your friend Thane Davis."

My heart softens as I think about the two of them meeting in person. "You will like him, *Mamulya*."

"If he is anything like you, I will love him."

I can imagine the power my mother's love could have on Thane, and I wish he'd visit sooner.

He should know and feel that kind of unconditional

love.

My mother peels and chops the eggs, throwing them into the beef and onion mixture. She then gets out the rolling pin and flours the marble slab before setting the dough on it. As she rolls out small balls of dough, she spoons in the meat mixture and seals up the edges.

Once all of them are made, she carefully places them in hot oil to fry. Soon the kitchen is filled with the smell of her fresh *piroshkis*.

Before they've had enough time to cool, I pick one up and take a bite. Although the heat of it burns my mouth, the savory beef and yeasty bread melds together making me groan in pleasure. "I've missed this…"

She grins. "I have, too."

Handing one to her, I command, "Partake with me."

I stare at my beautiful mother as the two of us quietly enjoy our labor of love. I realize that the only time I truly feel at home is when I'm by her side.

Return of the Knight

At my mother's insistence, I head out the next night to visit my favorite dungeon on the other side of Moscow. No one knows I'm here, so it should make for an interesting time when I show up unannounced.

The reputation I have at the LA dungeon is nothing compared to the one I have here in Russia. But, as I approach the imposing castle with the extensive dungeon in its basement, I'm overcome with a sense of loss.

I have to laugh at myself. It appears I've grown accustomed to having Thane and Anderson around whenever I scene and now I find it unnatural to be alone. Hell, I've changed more than I expected by going to America.

I use the large knocker on the heavy door to announce my arrival and stand back with my hands behind my back while I wait.

Ivanov, an older gentleman with a scar across his right cheek, opens the door and his eyes widen when he realizes who is standing before him. "Rytsar Durov?"

I smile, nodding.

"Come in! This is such an unexpected surprise. We were told you were in the US."

"I was, but not anymore," I answer, clapping him on the shoulder. "I must say it's good to be home, Ivanov."

He leads me through the grand entrance. Intricate patterns of inlaid wood cover the floor, while the white walls never fail to impress with their accents of real gold. He takes me to the dramatic staircase leading down to the dungeon.

This dungeon is different than most. Only families of distinction even know of its existence. The Durovs have long been respected among the social elite, so we are a welcomed addition to any gathering, but the fact that I am a skilled sadist also makes me highly sought after in this particular circle.

Ivanov opens the door to usher me inside, but I take a moment before entering to savor the unique scent of his castle dungeon. For some reason, it has an alluring smell that reminds me of old books mixed with a hint of cloves. I take in a deep breath, letting it enter my soul again after my long hiatus.

Ivanov waits patiently, but once I take a step through the door, he opens his mouth to announce my name. I put a finger to my lips and shake my head.

He quickly closes his mouth, nods and quietly closes the door behind me. A few people glance at me out of curiosity, but as soon as they recognize who I am, they put their tools down and openly stare. I walk through the immense room and observe the various scenes, but my presence causes an odd phenomenon. The lively dungeon becomes eerily quiet as I walk from one end to the other.

As the silence drags on, I grin and pound my chest as I boast loudly, "It's good to be home!"

A roar of agreement from my compatriots fills the dungeon.

"Return to your subs," I command. "I want to bask in their screams."

I'm moved when many of them do not obey, releasing their subs from their bonds instead and bringing them forward to kneel before me.

I stand with pride while I watch seven naked subs offer themselves to me. The protocol is strict here, so the submissives all kneel in the same position with their open palms up and heads bowed low.

I miss the enthusiastic greetings of my American submissives, but this particular community doesn't allow for that. A sub does not speak unless spoken to and will not make eye contact out of respect for the Dominant's status. That is the way it has always been here. I'll admit it took me a while to adjust to the more lax attitude at the dungeon in LA. However, there was a sense of openness there that I've come to appreciate.

Out of gratitude to each sub kneeling before me, I lightly touch the top of their heads as I go down the line. I recognize every one of them, including *malyshka*, whom I've scened with since I began as a young sadist looking to prove myself.

I cannot choose one amongst them, so I make the only sane choice—I choose them all.

"Stand and present yourselves at the wall."

The seven submissives stand up in unison, their gazes glued to the floor to avoid any hint of disrespect as they go to lay their hands on the rough, gray stone that makes up this ancient dungeon, spreading their legs apart.

Seven women of various body types, ages, and pain tolerances stand before me. I'm familiar with every one of them, and I stop to rub my hand over each sub's back before slapping her ass—the two areas I will be caressing with my 'nines. I call each sub by name and ask her about the level of impact she hopes to experience. I then kiss her on the lips before moving on to the next one.

Their Masters stand at a distance to watch this unusual scene play out. I nod to them, grateful for this gift they've given me.

This will be the first time I have ever scened with seven subs at one time, but I do not find it intimidating.

No, I find this challenge exhilarating.

I strip off my shirt and take my cat o' nines out of the bag.

I look down at my 'nines, smiling. Tonight, she is going to make many subs happy.

I start swinging her in the air, warming up the muscles that will be well used for this scene.

"First, I must remind you of her bite," I tell them. Going down the line, I deliver a demanding lash that causes each of the subs to cry out at the power behind the stroke.

Now that I have reacquainted them with her bite, I will let six of them wait in anticipation as I concentrate on the girl in front of me.

"Stand on your toes," I command.

She readjusts her position, standing on tiptoes, giving her legs an even more alluring appearance. However, the purpose of my command is to force her to concentrate on two things at once—the challenging lashes from my 'nines, as well as staying on her tiptoes during the entire session.

Zaika has asked for a level eight in intensity, so I deliver it to her, the first three strokes hitting that note before I change things up, varying the power of my stokes to keep her guessing. The tone of her cries changes from pain to pleasure as she begins to enter subspace.

When I pause to check her, she lets out a disappointed whimper.

Moving up to *zaika*, I reach between her legs and find her wet. I run my fingers over her clit, feeling her body tremble as she lets out a series of soft moans.

"Do you want me, *zaika?*" I growl in her ear.

"*Da*, Rytsar," she pants.

I kiss her on the cheek and move to the next sub.

Playing with each of them in this same way, I carry them into subspace but leave them desperate for more. My muscles ache from the effort, but I am well pleased as I stand back. I have seven subs dripping wet, flying in subspace, and greedy for a cock to claim them.

I turn to the Dominants who offered their subs to me and tell them to partake.

With great satisfaction, I watch each couple give into their carnal desire, fucking as they cry out in pleasure, their bodies becoming one.

I did this…

Looking around the dungeon, I notice a lone woman hiding behind a St Andrew's cross. I ask Ivanov about her and learn that she is a distant relative of his just recently introduced to the BDSM world.

"Would you be opposed if I interacted with her?"

His eyes flicker with unexpected concern. "She is new to this lifestyle and was not brought up as we were."

I smile, clapping him hard on the back. "I can be as gentle as I can be harsh."

Ivanov stares at me before nodding his approval.

As I walk over to the woman, I begin assessing her. She looks to be almost twenty years my senior, but I've found when it comes to sexual encounters, age has little relevance. It's a woman's inner confidence that I respond to.

Her blonde hair falls softly around her shoulders, but it's her kissable red lips that draw my attention. When she sees me approaching, she instantly falls to her knees with her head bowed.

"Do you want to be here?" I ask her.

She looks up at me with big brown eyes, clearly surprised by the question, then immediately averts her gaze, knowing she's just broken protocol.

"Yes," she answers meekly like a scared little mouse.

It brings out my protective side and I ask, "Why have you come?"

She lets out a soft sigh, keeping her eyes down. "I want more than I've experienced."

I gesture toward the expansive dungeon. "Is this what you really want?"

She nods. "I do, but…"

"But…what?" I lean down to lift her chin, so her gaze meets mine.

"I don't know if I can handle it," she whispers.

"I appreciate the honesty," I tell her, then ask, "Would you like to test it out?"

She raises her eyebrows in surprise.

"We can retire, away from prying eyes."

I notice that she swallows hard but says nothing.

"Are you afraid of me?"

Her face reddens and her hands tremble a little, but she nods yes.

I smirk. "You should be."

To ease her mind, I decide to make an unusual offer for a Master at this dungeon. "I will give you power tonight in the form of a safeword."

I can tell she is unfamiliar with the concept, so I answer her unspoken question. "You call out the word 'red' and I will stop, no questions asked."

She shakes her head, sounding concerned. "Is such a thing done here?"

"As your Master for the scene, what I say is all that matters to you."

I see a slight smile flit across her lips.

"You may fear me, but do you trust me?" I ask, holding my hand out to her.

I am gratified when she takes it and stands up. It is obvious she is not yet comfortable with her body by the way she hunches her shoulders, so I tell her, "Straighten your back and present yourself confidently to the world."

She immediately stands taller but remembers to keep

her eyes on the ground. I grunt my approval at the difference that simple change makes. "A Dominant is attracted to confidence. Never forget that."

"Yes, Master."

"My name is Rytsar."

She smiles and I question her, "What do you find amusing?"

"Nothing," she apologizes. "I was simply thinking you are a *rytsar* to me."

I chuckle lightly as I guide her out of the dungeon, saying, "One person's knight is another man's nightmare."

She squeezes my hand, keeping that confident stance as she walks. Ivanov looks at me appreciatively as he opens the door and offers any of his rooms to use.

I decide to take her to the library. The room is impressive, with a huge collection of books that cover every wall except one. That last wall has an impressive floor-to-ceiling fireplace, which is already crackling with a warm fire.

I stand behind her, caressing her soft skin while both of us stare at the flames. "Tonight, I will introduce you to pain in increments." I kiss one bare shoulder, then move to the other. "I will hurt you, but you will grow to like it."

Her breath comes a little faster.

"Is that what you are hoping to experience, *krasotka?*"

I've chosen to call her 'beauty', wanting to express my honest assessment of her.

I can tell she is pleased by the pet name because of

the rosy blush that rises on her cheeks.

"Put your hands up," I command her. She lifts her arms slowly, but I can already feel her fear.

She doesn't realize it is an aphrodisiac for me.

Breaking old traditions, I order her to look in my eyes while we scene. I want to see that fear play out on her face as I introduce her to the sensations I have planned.

I lightly caress the length of her arms, causing her to giggle as I pass by the ticklish parts. I continue downward to her breasts. "Do you like it when a man plays with your breasts?"

She nods.

I start playing with her nipples the way most men do, and she moans softly in pleasure. I then start tugging and pinching harder. "Does this feel good?"

She lets out a whimper of pleasure.

"Hold still and make no sound," I order as I pull and squeeze them with more focus.

She trembles against me but stays silent. As a reward, I begin kissing and nibbling her neck while continuing to play with her breasts, providing her with dual stimulation.

"For every pain, there is pleasure," I tell her. With my fingers still tugging at one nipple, my other hand moves between her legs to feel her bare mound.

She's still dry. All of this is too new for her body to respond to, so I wrap my hand around her throat as I seek out her lips. Kissing her possessively, I penetrate her mouth with my tongue.

She opens her lips, letting me kiss her more deeply.

I pinch her nipple again, causing her to whimper, while I explore her mouth. That turns me on, and I growl with animalistic desire.

Pressing my hard cock against her to let her know just how aroused I am, I continue to pinch her nipple as I explore her mouth. I could actually come from this simple stimulation, but I want more for both of us.

Reaching between her legs again, I feel the slippery evidence of her desire and groan in approval. Playing with her clit causes her to squirm against me, fanning the flames of my need.

"Do you want to please your Master?"

"Yes, Rytsar," she moans, pressing her pussy against my hand.

I slowly push her to her knees and undress in front of her, exposing my hard shaft. "Have you ever sucked cock before?"

She nods confidently.

"Have you ever deep-throated one?"

Her eyes grow wide as she answers apologetically, "*Nyet*, Rytsar."

I smile, glad to hear it. "Then let me be your first."

Opening her lips, she takes my cock into the silky warmth of her mouth and begins sucking.

"More," I command.

She enthusiastically takes more of my cock but chokes on it in her eagerness.

I fist her hair to help her with the depth and begin slowly thrusting into her mouth, allowing her throat to acclimate to the girth of my shaft. I have not had someone new to this in a long time and find it erotic to teach her body my needs.

I am patient with her as I instruct her to take more and more of my cock. Any second, I could thrust my cock deep in her throat and come, but I hold back.

"Look up at me," I order. Those big brown eyes immediately meet my gaze and I watch with pleasure as her lips travel down my cock almost to the base. I hold her there for several moments before setting her free. The next time, she takes me even deeper and I groan in pleasure.

"Good girl…"

She smiles with my cock still in her mouth and continues to make love to my cock with her throat.

When my balls start aching with an impending orgasm I pull away, needing to feel the tight caress of her pussy.

"Lay yourself against the arm of the leather chair and face the fire."

I want her to stare into the flames as I pound into her.

"Spread your legs wider," I command. I position myself behind her, kneeling on the floor. I will not be gentle when I fuck her, but I want her body to be ready for it, so I lean down and lick her clit.

She cries out in surprise, obviously not expecting my tongue. I have long practiced the art of cunnilingus, so it is not hard for me to bring a woman to orgasm. However, I insert my finger inside her to stroke her G-spot, wanting to feel her milk it when she comes.

It doesn't take long before *krasotka* starts moaning loudly, her orgasm imminent. It excites me and I increase the flicking of my tongue in rhythm with my finger. She suddenly stiffens, and then her pussy starts pulsing against my tongue while her inner muscles caress my finger with the strength of her climax.

After the last pulse subsides, I move into position to take her, slapping her hard on the ass.

She squeals with pleasure.

Rubbing my cock against her wet pussy, I tell her, "You will remember this claiming. You'll savor this moment when you surrendered your body to me, and I took complete control."

Looking back at me, her pupils widen with desire as I press the head of my cock against her opening.

"Ready?" I ask her.

"*Da*, Rytsar…" she says, moaning softly.

I plunge my cock into her, wanting *krasotka* to feel every centimeter of my shaft as it sinks into her.

Her moans suddenly stop as I force her body to take the fullness of my cock, but she soon starts crying out in passion when I begin to thrust. She is unusually pliable, obviously enjoying the deep penetration after her intense orgasm.

"Is this what you wanted to experience tonight?" I ask huskily.

"*Da*…" she pants.

"This is nothing."

I gather her hair in one hand and pull her head back while I grasp her waist with the other. "Prepare to be claimed," I state.

She whimpers in anticipation.

I close my eyes for a moment, gathering myself before I begin. I need to control the raging desire that threatens to send me over the edge.

Taking a deep breath, I tighten my grip on her waist and begin to thrust. I start out making each thrust deep, then switch the tempo up, stroking her faster and harder. Her panting soon become unintelligible screams as I let passion take over and pound her pussy hard.

I watch the flesh of her buttocks ripple with the impact of every stroke. That sensuous sound of skin slapping against skin fills the library as the raw smell of our sex teases my senses.

In that primal moment, I forget everything around me as I penetrate her deeply with my cock over and over again.

A chill runs through me when I've reached my limit.

Letting go of her hair, I grab her buttocks with both hands and let loose the beast inside as I fuck her like a jackhammer until I come.

The release is incredible, my balls aching painfully just before my cock pumps my seed deep into her. She cries out as she receives the stronger thrusts my body delivers at the end.

There is no other pleasure on Earth greater than this!

I pant afterward, worn out after such an intense climax. Slowly pulling from her, I watch my come spill from her swollen pussy and am hit with a feeling of manly satisfaction.

Exhausted, I get to my feet, needing to sit down. I pick her up by the waist and collapse into the chair with her on my lap.

She hasn't spoken a word, only moaning softly to

herself.

I nuzzle her ear before biting down on her neck, a symbolic claiming to end our session.

"Rytsar?" she whispers, her voice rough from screaming.

"*Da, krasotka?*"

"I'm still floating."

I chuckle, kissing her on the forehead.

Sitting there, listening to her soft breathing while I watch the flames dance on the log in the fireplace, I feel completely and utterly satiated.

Betrayed

My mother does not wake me the next morning, which is appreciated, considering how late it was when I returned after my night at the dungeon.

It turned out to be good reconnecting with my countrymen. Going there reminded me of who I once was and could be again.

As I roll out of bed, I notice the picture I drew of my mother. Taking it with me, I head to the kitchen where I hear her humming a favorite lullaby from my childhood.

I walk into the kitchen smiling at her. "I have missed hearing that."

Her eyes twinkle with delight as she looks up at me before going back to shaping the *syrniki* for breakfast.

"There is no reason to fuss over me," I scold her tenderly.

She laughs. "Don't take away my right to spoil you, Anton."

I love it whenever she says my name because she says it with such love. Some might say that I am a mama's boy, but the simple fact is that my mother is an extraordinary woman on every level—exceptionally beautiful, incredibly kind, highly intelligent and skilled in the kitchen. I am grateful that her blood runs through my veins.

"At least let me help, *Mamulya*."

She shoos me away, giggling. "You always burn the *syrniki*."

Sliding a cup over to me, she says, "Just sit back and drink your tea. I made it just the way you like it—one and a half teaspoons of sugar and a squeeze of lemon."

I take the cup of black tea smirking at her. "Fine, I'll pretend not to be insulted."

She lets out a peal of laughter that makes my heart flutter with joy.

I hand her the picture. "For you."

She wipes her hands on a towel before taking it from me. "Oh, Anton. This is beautiful."

I smile and say with all sincerity, "Because you're beautiful."

She blushes, looking back at the picture. "I don't think I've ever looked as beautiful as this, my son, but I'm flattered."

I chuckle. "Really, *Mamulya*? This is what I see every time I look at you."

Shaking her head, she gives me a peck on the cheek. "I will have it framed and cherish it forever."

While she goes back to making the *syrniki*, I slip a little vodka into my tea when she's not looking, then sit back to enjoy observing her skills in the kitchen.

I can actually imagine being happy again, making

sure my mother is well taken care of while I forge a new path like the one Thane has talked about.

In this moment, I feel as if anything is possible…

"What are you smiling about?" she asks as she sets the first batch into the pan and they start to sizzle.

"I will make you proud, *Mamulya.*"

She shakes her head, looking at me with amusement. "Silly boy, I'm already proud."

Tears well up in my eyes, so I take a quick sip of the tea to distract myself. "You want to know what's really funny?" I ask.

"What?" She sets the hot *syrniki* on a plate and slides them over to me.

I momentarily forget what I'm talking about and take a scoop of sour cream to plop on top of the golden-brown pancakes. I cut through the fluffy *syrniki* and take a big bite. Hmm…its light texture, along with the combination of sweet and tanginess from the sour cheese brings me back to my childhood—before the beatings began—and a genuine tear of happiness runs down my cheek.

"I bet you didn't know your *syrniki* could make a grown man cry."

She laughs and starts cooking another batch.

"There is no doubt you are going to blow Anderson's mother out of the water with your cooking—but, respectfully, of course."

She shakes her head with amusement, then asks, "What was that funny thing you wanted to tell me?"

I take another bite before answering, the *syrniki* too good to resist. "I was remembering the looks on my friends' faces when I introduced them to a dungeon for the first time."

Her eyes light up. "Tell me."

I chuckle as I think back on it. "They were equal parts shocked, offended, and intrigued."

My mother laughs. "Offended? How so?"

"They wanted to fight to protect all the ladies."

"That's very chivalrous of them," she giggles.

"Once I explained the women were there because they enjoyed it, it didn't take them long to embrace the BDSM lifestyle."

She looks at me with adoration. "What a gift you've given your friends."

I shrug. "It turned out I've learned a few things from them as well."

"Good friends will do that."

I lean my elbow on the table and smile at her. "I can't wait for you to meet them."

She reaches over and squeezes my hand. "I can't either, Anton."

I go back to eating my last remaining *syrniki* while she finishes cooking the final batch. "Do you remember that time when you and Titov staged that fake *bratva* shootout downtown and almost got yourselves killed?"

I burst out laughing, having forgotten that. "The police thought we really were the *bratva* and hauled us to jail. Imagine their surprise when our automatic rifles turned out to be painted broomsticks. It was epic!"

She shakes her head. "As funny as it was, it was a terribly dangerous stunt you two pulled."

I shrug, stating proudly, "We were only thirteen and

made the national news!"

"*Da*, but your father was extremely unhappy about it."

I remember his punishment like it was yesterday. He beat me to within an inch of my life, but it was the last time I ever let him touch me again…

"I wouldn't change a thing," I tell her.

"I'm just glad you survived all your crazy shenanigans with Titov."

I frown when I hear her mention his name again. My hatred for Titov has grown with each passing month since Tatianna's death. If he hadn't gotten involved with the *bratva*, she would still be alive.

"We don't speak of his name, remember?" I remind her.

She swirls her dollop of sour cream over her *syrniki* slowly. "He curses himself every day for what happened."

I stand up, roaring in anger. "And he should! He killed Tatianna because of his association with those lowlife scum. He may as well have handed her to the slavers himself."

My head starts to spin, and I can feel my blood pounding, so I sit back down and take several deep breaths to calm myself.

My mother walks over and wraps her arms around me, laying her cheek against mine. She is the only one who would dare to come near me in this state, but her touch soothes my soul and my racing heart quickly slows.

"I know her death devastates you."

A tear runs down my face and I nod.

"But, Titov loved his sister deeply, and the guilt he bears is killing him."

"Good," I snort in anger.

"Anton, he did not do this. What happened is purely on Yuri's shoulders."

"I don't want to hear it. I told him the *bratva* were bad news. I warned him."

She looks at me with compassion. "What if something had happened when you were playing your childish prank with broomsticks, and Titov had died because of it? Would you be to blame for his death?"

"Don't do this to me," I warn her. "I have every right to hate Titov. Every right!"

She smiles sadly. "Just know he hurts, too."

I do not want to feel any compassion toward Titov, so I shrug off her advice. "If you have any fault, it's that you are too kind."

When I see the hurt in her eyes, I instantly regret saying it. "I didn't mean that."

She nods but goes back to her seat and quietly finishes her breakfast.

My heart aches knowing I've hurt her. "I love you, *Mamulya*. More than you know."

Looking up at me with tears in her eyes, she smiles. "I love you too, Anton."

Offering her a figurative olive branch, I tell her, "Someday, I may find myself in a place where I can forgive him."

"And, I look forward to that day," she says, gracing me with a genuine smile.

Wanting to lighten her heart, I ask, "If you could do anything—anything at all—what would you want to do today?"

She blushes slightly. "It's simple."

"Tell me," I reply, interested to know her heart's desire.

"I'd like to look at old family photos with you."

I smirk. "I would take you anywhere and do anything with you, and that's what you choose?"

Her smile broadens. "*Da.*"

"Old photos it is, then."

We spend the entire day and well into the evening pouring over every photo album she can find. Some photographs go back to my great-great-great grandfather's time. She knows everyone's name and shares entertaining stories or interesting facts about each person in the numerous photos.

My mother is like a living encyclopedia of the Durovs, and she wasn't even born into our family. I stare at her in wonder, amazed that she carries so much knowledge about us.

"How do you know all this?"

"I have sought out every living relative within traveling distance and spent time talking about the family for hours."

"Why?" I ask, stunned to learn this.

"Because the Durovs are part of my boys' heritage."

I give her a hug, inspired by her deep love for her children. "You're amazing, *Mamulya.*"

She settles against me, smiling. "So are you, my son."

The phone rings, breaking our intimate moment. My

mother gets up to answer it and smiles as she hands the phone to me. "It's your friend, Sergei."

I frown, wondering why he's calling me here. We haven't spoken since the day I left for America.

"What's up, Sergei?" I ask stiffly.

"I just heard you're back in town and thought you should get drunk with the gang at our favorite bar. We're all curious to hear what America was like."

I quickly answer, "Not tonight."

My mother waves at me to get my attention, whispering, "What does he want?"

I cup my hand over the phone. "He wants me to hang with the guys. Nothing important."

She smiles. "I think you should go. It'll be good for you to spend time with your friends."

"Are you sure?" I ask, uncertain about leaving.

"It would make me happy," she answers with a twinkle in her eye.

My lips twitch in indecision, but I give into my mother's wishes and tell Sergei, "I'll meet you at Kamchatka tonight and, yes, I'll buy you that drink."

I snort in amusement as I hang up. "I suspect the only reason he called was to collect on that bet we made before I left."

"You're wrong." She caresses my cheek, looking at me lovingly. "I think you'd be surprised by how many of your friends have missed you. I'm glad to see you reconnect with them."

I shrug, admitting, "It will be good to see the gang and see what they are up to."

I throw on a black t-shirt and jeans before I head out

to the bar. "I'll try to get back at a more reasonable hour tonight."

She laughs. "I'm not worried."

I grab the keys, giving her one last hug before heading downstairs. "I'll tell Sergei you gave me a curfew."

Her laughter is the last thing I hear as I lock the front door behind me and walk to the car. I glance back at the house to see my mother standing at the window, waving down at me.

As I raise my hand up to wave back, the hairs on my neck begin to rise. I see the outline of someone approaching her from behind. With lightning speed, he grabs her around the waist and unceremoniously slits my mother's throat.

The man lets her fall to the floor and then looks out the window at me.

I run back to the door but have to fumble for the keys before I can unlock it. Even as I race up the stairs, I know I'm already too late to save her.

When I reach the room, I find my mother lying in a pool of red.

The assassin is gone and, as much as I want to chase him down to kill him, I go to comfort my mother instead.

Sinking to the floor, I gather her in my arms. The look of surprise on her face as she stares up at me does me in. I hold my hand against her throat but can't stop the blood that pours from her with each heartbeat.

"I love you, *Mamulya*," I tell her as my heart rips in two.

She looks up at me, trying to speak, but chokes on

her own blood. To comfort her as she dies, I sing the lullaby she used to sing to me when I was a boy.

My voice catches as I sing it to her.

Darkness is falling,
The moon will be rising
The stars will be shining
The sun's gone to sleep
Close your eyes
And I'll rock you gently
And wish you sweet dreams
While you sleep
Good night,
Good night
Now it is time to sleep.

Tears stream down my face as the light fades in her eyes and I feel her spirit leave.

Closing her eyelids, I cradle her body against mine, rocking her as I moan with uncontrollable grief.

My sweet *mamulya* is dead.

Terrifying Truth

I only see red…

I leave my mother, my clothes drenched in her blood, to seek out the man responsible for this. With no thought for myself, I speed toward Koslov headquarters, knowing that is where I will find him.

I am bent on avenging my mother's death at any cost and break through their security with minimal effort, the sight of me striking terror in the hearts of Koslov's men.

I demand to see Vladimir Durov.

Seeing I am covered in blood, and not wanting to add his own to the mix, a nervous guard offers to take me directly to him. I follow him down the corridors to a gambling area where I find my father sitting at a poker table with a large stack of chips in front of him.

The sight of him incenses me and I roar like a deranged lion.

He looks up from his cards and freezes when he sees me.

"You did this!" I yell.

He drops his cards and stands up, sputtering as he looks around at the others for help. "What…what…are you doing here?"

I stare him in the eye and say with deadly certainty, "I'm here to kill you."

My father steps back as several of Koslov's men move in front of him with their guns drawn, acting as a barrier against my impending fury.

Their effort is pointless—nothing will stop me from killing him.

"Why did you send an assassin for your wife?" I demand, wanting that question answered before I rip out his throat with my own teeth.

"I don't know what you are talking about…!" he cries in terror, moving further away from me.

The fact that he isn't surprised or asks about what has happened to her only confirms his guilt.

"She loved you. She was loyal to you! Why the fuck would you kill her?"

Rather than answer my question, he cries out to the Koslov men, "You can't shoot him."

If he foolishly thinks that will save his life, he's mistaken. It only angers me more. "You killed her, and for that, you must die. But I will *not* be as quick."

When I step forward, Koslov's men ready their guns, but my father screams again, "You can't kill him!"

I laugh like a lunatic, intent on ripping my father to pieces no matter how many men must die in the process.

"Stop!"

I turn to see the Koslov brothers, Gavriil and Stas, standing in the doorway.

"Do not make another move toward him," Gavriil warns me.

I glare at the fool, having zero respect for him. "You have no say in this."

"But we do," his boyish brother sneers.

"How?" I demand of Gavriil, ignoring Stas completely.

"Vladimir has paid his debt in full," he says with a cold smile.

A chill runs down my spine.

I turn to my father in a rage. "She died for your gambling debt?"

The blood in my veins starts pumping furiously as my vision starts to blur.

The great Vladimir, feared by many, now cowers behind a wall of men. I can smell his fear.

We both know we are going to die tonight.

I only see red as I rush toward Koslov's men, screaming my battle cry. My lethal fists meet flesh and bone as I let the berserker inside have free reign over me...

I wake up in pain.

My body feels as if it's been put through a meat grinder.

I blink several times before turning my head and am surprised to see Nikolay, the Koslov *Pakhan*. My brain can't fathom why the head of the Koslov organization would be sitting across from me, but I know I'm in danger.

Despite the pain, I bolt up from the couch, crouching defensively, my fight instinct kicking in as I glance around the room for possible attackers.

But we are alone.

I put my fists down and glare at Nikolay, wondering why he has brought me here.

"You are a bull when you lose your mind, Anton. It took eight of my men to finally take you down, and that was after you incapacitated five of them."

I ask him the only question that matters. "Did I kill him?"

"Who? Your father?"

I say nothing. It is a foolish question.

Nikolay smiles casually. "Thankfully not, because I would not have been able to save you, if you had." He goes on to explain, "My grandsons are very possessive of your father for some unfathomable reason."

I suspect that my father is a pawn in some sick, twisted game of theirs, but it was my sweet mother who suffered for it. I feel the unbearable ache return knowing she is gone, and I close my eyes to keep the tears from falling in front of the *Pakhan.*

"Unfortunately, my men paid the price protecting him from you," Nikolay complains.

It makes no sense to me that the Koslovs would risk their men for Vladimir Durov, and I question him on it. "Why are you protecting my father?"

Nikolay presses his fingers together thoughtfully, taking his time to answer. "My grandsons have an unusual attachment to your father that I do not care for but, once they publicly announced that he was under the protection of the Koslovs, I unwillingly became duty-bound to see that he remains unharmed. To allow Vladimir to die would be a mark against our family. I cannot allow that as *Pakhan*."

"You should have let me kill him!"

He meets my gaze and says simply, "I did not want to see you die."

Nikolay's answer surprises me and I instantly become suspicious. Am I just another pawn to get back at his unruly grandsons? I refuse to be played and demand, "Why? I am nothing to you."

He smiles. "Did your grandfather ever speak of me?"

I do remember my grandfather mentioning Nikolay on several occasions and answer with the truth, even though the *Pakhan* may find it insulting. "He told me he respected you…despite your connection to the *bratva*."

Chuckling, Nikolay replies, "He and I have always had a mutual respect for each other, yes. What I admired in him, I see in you. It is the reason I ordered a stay of execution and had them bring you to my chambers."

My heart starts racing wondering if he plans to kill me without giving me the satisfaction of taking my father out. "Am I your prisoner just waiting for my own death?"

Nikolay stands up. He is an extremely tall man and towers over me, but I am not intimidated by his stature. I could still take him down.

"No, Anton. You are not a prisoner here. You can leave right now, if you wish. However, you should know that my grandsons want you dead and there will come a time when I will not be able to prevent it."

"Because?" I demand.

Nikolay looks away, saying in a resigned voice, "I will pass on to the other side and whether I want it or not, they will become the new ruling power over the Koslovs."

"Those two are worthless. Unworthy of the Koslov name," I protest.

He nods. "I agree."

My eyes narrow. No *Pakhan* would ever admit to such a thing. "Why would you say that when they are your kin?"

He shrugs. "It's no different than you and your father. We do not choose our bloodline. Sometimes nature makes a mistake—or, in my case, two."

I snort, agreeing with his assessment.

When his expression grows serious, I realize I'm about to discover the true reason I've been brought here.

"Your grandfather found himself in the same predicament I find myself in now. But, unlike me, who has no one else to choose from, he was able to pass over his son when it came time to grant his inheritance to someone."

I shake my head. What game is he trying to play? I'm not a fool like his grandsons and growl, "This is utter nonsense!"

He looks at me gravely. "When your grandfather gave you his ring, he passed on everything he had to you."

I look down at the gold ring with the black dragon and huff, stating sarcastically, "Why was I not made aware of this?"

He raises an eyebrow, telling me, "Being a highly intelligent individual, your grandfather always had a method to his madness."

He looks at the ring again. "Although your father knows exactly what that ring on your finger represents, few others do. I suspect your grandfather wanted you to live out your youth unencumbered by the responsibility such immense wealth would bring."

I throw back my head and laugh sarcastically. "*That* is the reason you spared me? You want his money?"

"I have no interest in your inheritance," Nikolay replies, clearly insulted.

I fold my arms together, snorting in disbelief. "I find it very odd that I was not made aware of this."

"You've been living off a portion of that inheritance since your grandfather died. Have you never questioned the source?"

I shrug. "I assumed it was funded by the inheritance, but the allowance came directly from my father."

"Sneaky bastard," Nikolay mutters under his breath, shaking his head.

I uncross my arms, spreading them wide as I laugh. "So, are you trying to claim that all this time, I have been rich but didn't know it?"

Nikolay gazes at me, thinking for a moment before stating, "There must be an age clause set in his will."

An age clause?

All of this is getting too farfetched, but he has entertained me so far, so I bait him to continue by asking, "What do you mean?"

"The full inheritance will not be yours until a stipulated age. At the age your grandfather deemed you would be old enough to control the power behind such wealth."

I shake my head in disbelief. "If that is true, why would my father lead me to believe the inheritance had been passed down to him instead?"

"Such blatant deceit speaks to his hidden motive."

Nikolay now has my full attention. Nothing involving my father is ever good. "What are you saying?"

"I firmly believe Vladimir hoped you would instigate your own demise. It's the only way the inheritance would end up in his hands."

I suddenly feel the hairs rise on my neck.

"What exactly are you implying?" I demand.

"Your grandfather's inheritance would automatically revert to his only son should you commit suicide. If your father could keep you ignorant of your wealth, it would give him significant leverage to begin stripping away your will to live."

A horrifying thought flashes through my head as I process what he's saying. My grandfather had given me the ring just two months before I started courting Tatianna…

My heart starts pounding. "It's not possible."

The idea of this is too horrendous. I have openly hated Titov this entire time for his involvement with the *bratva* because it led to Tatianna's death.

But…what if her kidnapping had *not* been Titov's fault?

A cold chill runs through me as I think back on that

day when Titov came banging on my door.

Yuri was the one who sold her to pay off his gambling debt, but I never saw that maggot again, even though I tried unsuccessfully to hunt him down. I've always assumed he went into hiding because he knew he was a dead man. But what if…

What if Vladimir had Yuri killed to eliminate any evidence that he was behind Tatianna's kidnapping?

I struggle to breathe.

If having me commit suicide has always been my father's intention, then he had come dangerously close to succeeding. I'd wanted to follow Tatianna after she committed suicide.

It was only my mother's insistence that I leave for America that prevented me from following through back then.

And now, she is dead.

Oh, God…

They are both dead because of me.

"You should have let me kill him!" I cry out in rage.

Nikolay keeps his calm demeanor, stating, "You already know why I could not."

I glare at him with a hatred so deep that it suffocates me. "I am *not* grateful to be alive today. I owe you nothing but my wrath at the injustice your interference has caused."

Raising an eyebrow, he answers, "I do not expect your gratitude."

"Then why am I here? What the hell do you want from me?" Tears of rage well up in my eyes.

When Nikolay gives me a look of compassion, I fight

the urge to wipe it from his face with my fist.

"Let me be completely frank with you." He moves closer, resting his hand on my shoulder. "Your father is unworthy of the power your grandfather's inheritance will give him. I prefer it goes to the man it was meant for."

"Why would you care?" I spit angrily.

He squeezes my shoulder. "Like I said, your grandfather and I respected each other. My profound respect for him extends to you."

I narrow my eyes, giving him the bad news. "Whether you like it or not, my father *will* die."

"As long as it's of 'natural causes', I have no issues with that."

I realize Nikolay is giving me permission to kill Vladimir in a manner that won't raise suspicion. As long as I am the one to end his life, I have no problem with that.

"I will see to it that Vladimir Durov dies a slow, painful, and humiliating death—by natural causes, of course," I tell him.

"Good."

Nikolay snaps his fingers and one of his men enters the room. "Rytsar Durov must be leaving. See to it that he gets to his destination safely."

"*Da, Pakhan.*"

I look at Nikolay realizing that he has not only opened my eyes to the truth but has also given me the opportunity to make things "right' with my father. Had I not known then what I know now, I would have killed the vile wretch without understanding the full extent of his crimes.

Now, I can give him the kind of death he deserves—from one sadist to another.

I hold out my hand to Nikolay. "Thank you."

He shakes it firmly, stating, "Lead the Durov family well."

I nod.

As I'm escorted out of the room, I turn back and tell Nikolay, "Don't die overly soon."

He smirks. "Goodbye, Anton Durov, grandson of Fedor Durov."

As I leave the Koslov headquarters, I feel the open stares of everyone I pass. Even though I can't remember what happened last night, the fearful looks in their eyes suggest I've left an impression none of them will forget.

That will serve me well.

Reconciliation

I am in a state of shock as I drive away, and the only place I can think to go is Titov's. As I pull up to his place, the conversation I had with my mother just yesterday pops into my head.

"I have every right to hate Titov. Every right!"

"Just know he hurts, too."

Tears run down my face unheeded.

Oh, Mamulya…

"I was wrong. I was so horribly wrong," I cry out.

I had no idea who the real danger was—and it wasn't Titov.

I wipe away my tears as I get out of the car. After taking several deep breaths, I walk up to his porch to ring the doorbell.

When Titov opens the door, he immediately frowns, his eyes set in an angry glare. "I have nothing to say, and seeing you only brings me pain." He shoos me away. "Go away, Rytsar."

I grab his arm and hold him in place. "I was wrong."

He stares at me, confused and surprised by my admission.

"I was wrong to blame you for Tatianna."

He shakes his head, looking bereft. "*Nyet.* You are right. My association with Yuri caused her death, and I will never forgive myself for that."

I see the devastation in his eyes as he thinks back on the tragic events leading up to his sister's death and it's clear he is suffering as much as I am.

"Can I come inside? I have something I need to tell you."

Titov seems startled by my request, but steps aside to let me in. We sit down at his small kitchen table and I stare him straight in the eye. "Would you like to help me kill the man who *is* to blame for her death?"

His jaw drops. "What? Did you finally locate Yuri?"

Shaking my head, I inform him, "I suspect Yuri is already dead."

"Who, then?" Titov demands, his anger pushing him to stand back up.

I clinch my fists as I admit the terrible truth out loud. "It was my father."

Titov's face goes white. "What?"

"Not only is Tatianna dead because of him but…now my mother is, too." I choke out the last few words, barely reigning in my grief.

"What is this? You're telling me that your mother is dead?" Titov cries, tears coming to his eyes.

I state the facts devoid of any emotion. "An assassin came last night as payment for my father's gambling debt. Does that sound familiar to you?"

Titov's eyes widen. He understands what that implies, but then he shakes his head, not believing it. "No…how can she be dead?"

I close my eyes, fighting against the grief that threatens to consume me. His walks over and I suddenly feel his stiff arms around me. "I'm so sorry for your loss, Anton."

I'm not prepared for his sympathy, and I do not return the embrace. I'm afraid if I do, I won't be able to control my emotions, so I simply endure it.

After he lets go, he sits back down. I can see he's visibly shaken by the news.

"My father is responsible for both of their deaths."

"But why?" he demands. "Why would he want them killed?"

I have blamed Titov for years, but the irony is that *I* am to blame for Tatianna's death. It was her association with me that spelled her doom. He may come to hate me once he knows, but he deserves to hear the truth from me.

"I recently learned that I am the one receiving my grandfather's inheritance. My father lusts after the money but can only lay claim to it if I die."

"Then why not simply kill you?" Titov asks bluntly.

I let out a long, heavy sigh. "Suicide is the only way it will revert to him, but there can be no hint that I was murdered."

Titov stares as me as he processes the news. He shakes his head again, tears coming to his eyes. "Why my sister?"

"My father knew I loved her, and he hoped that by

destroying her, he could get his way. It was a shrewd and heartless plan." Tears fill my own eyes and I growl. "I now have lost the two most important women in my life because of him, and I demand revenge."

He stands up quickly, pushing his chair backward. "Then why are we still here? He needs to die now!"

I gesture to Titov to sit back down. "I attempted to kill him last night but was stopped by Nikolay."

"Why would the Koslovs care?" Titov snarls, angry that we are still talking instead of leaving to kill my father.

"Titov, the brothers have granted my father their protection."

He furrows his brow as reality starts to set in. "But shouldn't you be dead then?"

I nod. "Nikolay spared my life because he agrees my father should die."

Knowing that we have the blessing of the Koslov *Pakhan*, Titov immediately asks, "What do you want me to do?"

I smirk, grateful for his offer to help. "I want you to secure some ricin."

"Poison?" he growls. "I want to rip him apart limb by limb! Where is the satisfaction in that? I *need* him to feel my wrath."

"I understand, Titov, and I promise he *will* feel your wrath, but it must appear that he died of natural causes. It is the only way Nikolay can condone his death without interfering."

"It's not good enough!"

"Look at me," I command. Gazing deep into his

eyes, I vow, "I promise you—it will be."

Letting out a ragged sigh, Titov agrees to it, albeit resentfully. "Fine. I trust you but I do *not* like it."

I look away as the scene of my mother's violent death suddenly replays in my head. It's still too fresh for me to shut it out, and I inadvertently let out an agonized groan.

Titov's expression suddenly changes to one of sympathy. "I'm gutted to hear about your mother's death. She was a kind woman and was a comfort to our family after Tatianna died."

My heart hurts even more knowing she gave solace to Titov and his family, while I only rained curses down on him.

"I grieve with you," he states quietly as a tear runs down his cheek.

I nod, getting up and seeing myself out.

I drive to my oldest brother's home. I'm not looking forward to telling my brothers what's happened but, like Titov, they need to know the truth.

The truth of who our father really is…

Vlad is shocked to see me standing there when he opens the door. I immediately notice that his eyes are red from crying. I'm relieved to know I won't have to inform him about our mother's death—on top of the terrible truth I must share.

"I need to talk to all of you, now," I tell him, after he

invites me inside.

"What's wrong? What more bad luck could fall on this family?" he growls, looking unsettled.

"I don't want to say until all of us are gathered."

Vlad calls to his wife and tells her to bring a bottle of vodka. "I'll make the calls."

I sit, downing two shots while I wait. When I see him again, I hand him the glass I've poured for him.

"So, I heard you were there," he states, his voice gruff with emotion.

I only nod, unable to speak of it.

"I can't imagine…"

He tips the glass, downing the shot, and I pour us both another. We sit in silence until the others arrive.

"Okay, what's this all about?" Andrev demands once Pavel and Timur have arrived.

I take a deep breath, retreating to simple facts when I describe how our mother died.

"Who would do such a thing?" Pavel, the youngest and most sensitive of the five of us, cries. "Everyone loved our mother."

"I know," I tell him.

"Why are we just standing here? Let's take the assassin out!" Vlad declares.

"Before we do anything, there is something I must tell you."

I pour them each another shot. I look each one of them in the eye before I voice the ugly truth. "It was our father who sent the assassin to kill her."

Vlad stands up and points at me, snarling, "Liar!"

"I understand how you feel, Vlad. I am as shocked as

you are, but it doesn't change the fact that our father had our beautiful mother killed…" My voice catches and I swallow down another shot to keep from crying.

"I don't believe it," Vlad declares.

Pavel agrees with him, insisting, "Father would never hurt Mama."

"What possible reason would he have to do such a thing? It was obviously a hit by the Koslovs or did you not know that?" Andrev asks with a distrustful sneer.

When even Timur, the most reasonable of my brothers, doesn't believe me, I look at them all in disgust.

"It was for money!" I tell them. "Our sweet mother died because Vladimir is a greedy bastard."

"That makes no sense!" Vlad states. "Our father is a rich man."

"There *are* rumors floating around that Father has amassed a sizeable debt because of his gambling habit," Timur offers, looking at me.

At least he is willing to listen to reason, unlike my oldest brother.

I nod. "I confronted him at the Koslov headquarters last night, Timur. I had every intention of killing Vladimir with my own two hands—"

"It is a cold day in hell when a son attacks his own flesh and blood," Andrev growls, shaking his head in disgust.

"Did you know Grandfather passed our father over when he allotted his inheritance, Andrev?" I shoot back. "Our father killed her in an attempt to get it back."

"What? Do the Koslovs have it now?" Pavel asks, looking at everyone in concern.

"No, you idiot," Vlad hisses, glaring at me. "Grandfather always had a favorite, didn't he?" He glances down at the ring on my finger with resentment. "I wouldn't be surprised if the old man gave it to you. He always treated you better than the rest of us."

"This isn't about who the favorite is," I snarl. "This is about the man who killed our mother."

Vlad shrugs, saying with disdain, "If what you say is true, why didn't Father kill you? He loves our mother. He always has."

"What? Are you saying Anton has all the money?" Andrev shouts angrily.

"I don't have it…yet," I tell him, before addressing Vlad. "Father can't claim the inheritance by killing me."

Pavel presses his fingers against his temples and starts rocking back and forth. "None of this is making sense." Tears roll down his cheeks and he whimpers, "Mama is dead…why are we fighting?"

"Because our father was the one who killed her!" I roar. "Why don't any of you care? The man needs to die."

Andrev stares at me suspiciously. "What if this is some crazy scheme of yours to steal the inheritance from Father?"

"Why would I do that? I don't want the money," I snarl.

"Because you hate Father. You always have!"

"Do I hate the man who tied me to the pole and whipped me repeatedly as a boy? Of course, I fucking do. But I would never kill him unless he hurt the person closest to me—to all of us."

"Your accusations are unfounded," Vlad states plainly. "There is no reason to believe what you say."

"Nikolay all but confirmed it today while I was at the Koslovs' headquarters. It's the only reason I'm still alive."

Timur looks at me with a thoughtful expression but says nothing.

"I refuse to believe Father did this," Pavel exclaims.

Andrev spits on the floor. "Everyone always favored you. Mama, Grandfather…even Father. And now you want to kill him?"

"Are you insane, Andrev? I would have traded places with you in a second rather than be forced to endure Father's sadistic brand of 'affection'."

"In the end, our mother is gone. Nothing we do will bring her back," Timur states in a calm voice. "I agree with Pavel. There is no reason for us to fight."

I shake my head in utter disbelief. "What is wrong with you? You all want Father to live after killing our mother?"

"As I said," Vlad replies in a cold tone, "what you are proposing is pure speculation. How unjust would it be if we killed our father and you turned out to be wrong?" He lifts his chin, looking down his nose at me. "I think you have held on to your resentment for so long that you are now blinded by it."

"I am not seeking revenge for myself. This is for *Mamulya*. Do none of you care?" I scream, horrified by the passivity of my brothers.

Pavel sniffles, wiping away his tears. "Of course, we care. We need to honor Mama as she would have wanted. We all need to grieve her loss as a family. Don't try to ruin this for us or her, Anton."

"How could you stand beside Father, knowing he is the reason she died such a violent death?" I ask in disbelief.

"In this case, it's your word against his. I personally would believe Father over you any day," Vlad answers coldly.

Timur glances at me, looking torn. "Brother, we must unite as a family. I don't want to hear any more discussion about Father murdering Mama. It's not only cruel but grossly untrue."

"Timur, you can't turn a blind eye to the truth. It's not fair to *Mamulya!*"

Andrev announces, "There will be a service for Mama tomorrow." Looking at me he states, "You are not invited to join us."

My other brothers all nod in agreement.

I stand up, backing away from them, horrified by this unexpected turn of events.

They are all sniveling cowards, just like my father. It seems I am the only one with any backbone and a sense of justice.

"I would never stand in mourning next to the man who murdered her. You are all dead to me!"

I slam the door on my way out, feeling completely numb inside.

The fact that my brothers are as spineless as my father rocks me to the core. We may all look the same, but my brothers lack his sadistic nature.

No, that has been passed down to me, and I will have no trouble dealing out the kind of justice my father deserves.

Rescue

I go to my mother's grave late in the day, after the graveside service is over and everyone in attendance has left.

My heart contracts when I see the fresh mound of dirt.

It makes it real.

I will never look on her face again in this lifetime.

I set the bouquet of chamomile on the mound. They were her favorite flower. Forty-two of them—one for each year of her life.

"Mamulya..." I cry out looking up to the heavens. The sky is filled with dark clouds, which seems appropriate—the world should weep for the loss of my mother.

I'm consumed by a mix of emotions—the guilt of not being able to protect her, the sorrow of losing such an extraordinary woman, anger at the violence of her death, a longing for justice and the profound grief a man has over losing his mother.

Feeling the first drop of cold rain, I nod, realizing

that I am not alone. The sky above me expresses my grief in the form of a raging storm. I stand in it, my tears hidden by the drenching rain.

Closing my eyes, I extend my arms out while the winds buffet me. I mourn with nature over the loss of such a beautiful soul…

Afterward, I head to the family estate and wait in the car. I watch as my father leaves with an attractive young woman by his side.

I clench my fists, enraged that he would dare do such a thing on the day of my mother's funeral. But there is nothing decent about the man.

The only thing keeping me from jumping out of the car and beating him to death is the knowledge that I *must* remain patient when exacting a revenge of this nature.

Once he drives off, I walk up to my ancestral home and let myself in. One look at my drenched clothes has the staff moving into action. A bath is drawn, dry clothes set out, while the cook, Nadia, quickly whips something up for me in the kitchen.

Unlike my father, I am well loved by the staff here, as was my mother. I notice their red-rimmed eyes and know they are mourning her death just as I am.

I can feel their silent resentment toward my father for his actions tonight. The open disrespect toward my mother's memory is shocking. If they knew the truth about what happened, my father would have a mutiny on his hands.

Vladimir rules this house with an iron first. He is not fair, and his punishments are unusual and cruel. Only the loving touch of my mother kept the balance in this place.

Without her, this home has no heart.

I insist on eating what Nadia has made in the kitchen and call for more vodka as all of us begin sharing memories of my mother. In a time of great sorrow, we find solace in each other, remembering the joy she brought to our lives.

For a few precious hours, I feel no pain.

I want revenge, but without Tatianna and my mother in my life, I am struggling to survive. The pain of having to live each day without them is wearing on my soul.

The inheritance means nothing to me, while the allure of death continues to call with its sweet promise. More than anything, I long to be in their presence again.

I have made a vow to Thane so I continue to go through the motions, but I feel nothing now, and my soul is slowly dying.

I don't want this life anymore.

I take to the streets of Moscow, visiting taverns and bars, drinking vodka and picking fights. I am a ball of rage that needs release, so I take it out on those I see abusing their power—the man who hits his wife for spilling his drink, the drug addict who kicks a panhandler sleeping on the ground, a gang of boys mugging an old woman. No one is safe from me, and my body keeps paying the price. Bruises cover every inch of it and two of my ribs hurt so badly that it's difficult to breathe.

But I can't stop,

When I notice the Koslov men trailing me, I don't run. I stop and challenge them. "You want to off me? Now's your chance."

They make no move toward me and say nothing. I find it frustrating as hell and slam my fist into a brick wall. My hand explodes in pain, but I prefer that than to not feel anything at all.

I wipe the blood on my shirt and drop in the nearest bar to order a bottle of vodka. Chugging down my liquid escape, I stare at my reflection in the mirror behind the bar.

I look like death walking and that's exactly how I feel.

Glancing around the place, I notice a single woman nursing a beer. She doesn't belong in such a seedy establishment. The woman seems lost in her own thoughts, oblivious to everyone around her.

I then turn my attention to the waitress. Some may not consider her comely, but I see how hard she is working and how the people respond to her smiles and jokes, and that makes her beautiful in my eyes.

The world needs more people like her.

I raise my bottle to the waitress and toast her. "To a beautiful woman. May you continually find happiness."

She laughs self-consciously, shaking her head as she cleans off one of the tables. She probably thinks I'm drunk, but I have never been more clearheaded.

I get up, leaving the partially empty bottle, and give the waitress all my cash as a tip. She looks at me strangely, then tries to hand it back. "You need to eat."

I laugh, picking up the bottle to take one last drink.

"This is all this Russian needs."

As I leave, two men walk in, brushing past me. The instant we make contact I get a bad feeling, so I linger at the door while they sit down at the bar and start making lewd comments to the waitress. She handles it well, using humorous comebacks to stave them off.

After the two down a shot, they catch sight of the woman sitting alone at the table. Elbowing each other, they get up and walk over to her table.

I stiffen as they approach her.

"Hey princess, what's a fine woman like you doing alone?"

She looks up from her beer nervously, apparently too shy to speak.

One of them has the audacity to sit down next to her while asking, "You don't mind if I sit here, do you?"

"But I do," she answers meekly.

The other man ignores her answer, sitting down on the other side of her. He reaches out to touch a curl of her hair. "Don't be that way, pretty thing."

She moves to avoid his reach and tells them nervously, "I…I'm waiting for someone."

"We'll keep you company until he shows up."

One of the men calls out to the waitress, "Get us three shots. No, make it four." He looks at the woman again, stating, "She looks like she needs to loosen up."

I start moving toward them, catching the woman's eye.

She waves at me and says to them, "That's the guy I was waiting for."

I approach, assessing both men while I decide which

one to take out first if they prove to be a nuisance.

The two men look at me and start laughing. "What, baldy boy here?"

I smile—the kind of smile that means only trouble.

Both men stand up at the same time, trying to look intimidating.

Crossing my arms, I tell them, "Leave, before someone gets hurt."

They look at each other and laugh again just before first guy tries to sucker punch me.

I'm ready for it and dodge to the right while landing a solid hit to his nose. He screams in pain as his blood starts to run.

This enrages the second guy, who then jumps me. I swing him around and push him up to the wall, smashing him hard against it. With the wind knocked out of him, he falls to the floor, wheezing as he gasps for breath.

"We don't want any fights here," the waitress warns us.

I look down at Wheezer and say, "I have no issue taking it outside."

The one with the bloody nose helps Wheezer up from the floor and they both glare at me. "We're not going anywhere. We saw her first."

"She wants nothing to do with you," I tell them.

"Sure, she does," he replies, giving her a lustful look.

"You touch her, and I will kill you."

"You two leave now. Your business isn't wanted here," the bartender says, standing beside me.

Wheezer looks at him smugly. "We refuse to waste our rubles in this dive anyway."

As the two leave, Wheezer winks at the woman at the table and offers a veiled threat. "Next time, princess."

Once they're gone, everyone goes back to their drinks.

"Thank you for helping me," the woman says from the table, her fingers white from clutching her beer so tightly.

"It was nothing," I grunt in answer.

My blood is still pounding from having it out with those men. I nod to the waitress and step outside, blinking several times. The transition from the dark tavern to the bright sun makes it difficult for my eyes to adjust.

It allows just enough distraction that I'm unprepared for the hard kick to my groin. As I double over in pain, Wheezer and Bloody Nose drag me into an alley. Bloody pins my arms behind my back while Wheezer pummels me over and over.

When he finally gets tired, Bloody releases his hold and I collapse to the ground, puking from the multiple gut shots.

"That'll teach you to mess with us," Bloody says, wiping his nose.

As they walk off, I roll over and slowly get back up to my feet. "We're not done here."

They both turn around and laugh at me. "Oh, I'd say you're done," Wheezer says.

I smile, despite the pain of my split lip. With a rush of blood filling my ears, my vision starts to blur, and everything turns red…

I hear the agonized cries of both men as if from a distance and send a silent prayer to the God of the Universe.

Let this be the last. Take me home…

"Wake up. It's Thane. I'm going to get you out of here, but I need you to wake up, now!"

I don't trust the demons in my head and choose to sink back down into the darkness.

I hear a low whistle and another voice says, "You must have a death wish. Don't say I didn't warn you…"

Someone shakes me.

The pain that motion causes insights an instant reaction, and I hit my attacker square in the jaw.

He grabs my wrists and pins them to the ground.

I'm too dazed to hear what he's saying until I detect through the blur of noise two words "your brother".

I open my eyes and croak, *"Moy droog?"* My throat feels as if it's being pricked by a thousand tiny needles.

The realization that Thane is here, seeing me in this sorry state, fills me with shame and I turn my head. I command him to go and try to retreat back into the darkness.

"Like hell I will," Thane growls in my ear. He tortures me by throwing me over his shoulder. I'm jostled about, enduring intense pain until I'm finally deposited, fully clothed, into a bathtub.

I feel Thane's hands on me as he begins undressing

me, before turning the water on. The warm embrace of the water revives me, and I force my eyes open again.

I look up at Thane, the grief of my mother's death still too recent to hide from him.

When he looks away, I'm sure he's ashamed of me. I need him to leave so that death can finally have its way.

Instead, he cleans me up, washing every wound thoroughly. I lay there, feeling like I did the night he found me after Samantha's assault.

It is humiliating and I can't help resenting it.

Once he's done, Thane helps me to the bed and dials the phone to order food.

While we wait, the silence builds around us, but I have nothing to say.

"We're in this life together, no matter how bad it gets," he states, finally breaking the silence.

I turn my head away from him, embittered by that vow we made.

When the soup is delivered, Thane tries to feed me. After several failed attempts to force the soup into my mouth, I grumble. "What is this? A form of Chinese water torture, but with soup?"

"I need you to eat, damn it! So, you can either let me continue to treat you like a spoiled aristocrat or you can pick up the damn spoon and feed yourself. It's totally up to you but, either way, this soup is going down your throat."

I growl as I sit up and take the spoon from him. "You've always been a pain in my ass, peasant."

I can feel Thane's eyes on me as I eat. I want to stop, but the lemony tanginess of sorrel mixed with the vegetable broth is too good to deny.

It was a favorite dish of mine, one my mother made…but while the soup feeds my body, the memories tear at my soul, and I throw the spoon across the room once I'm done.

Thane picks it up, asking. "Did that make you feel better? If so, feel free to chuck it again."

I glare at him, wanting to deck him hard in the face. However, grief wins over and I confess, "I failed her. I shouldn't be here."

"What are you talking about? Tatianna would want you to live."

"I need to kill my father. I know he killed *Mamul-ya*…"

Thane looks at me in shock. "Your mother is dead?"

I nod, almost telling him the secret of Vladimir's true motives, but I stop myself. It is the one secret I will not share with him. The shame of knowing that I am ulti-mately the reason for their deaths will haunt me to my grave.

However, the grief I feel is too profound to suppress and I cry out in pain. "The bastard sacrificed my mother for a gambling debt."

Thane looks at me in horror. "How could he?"

I spit in disgust. "I went to kill him but was stopped from avenging my mother. Nikolay spared his life—and mine."

"I've heard that name mentioned several times today. Who is he?"

"The *Pakhan* of the Koslovs, a powerful clan in Rus-sia."

"So, he's part of the *bratva*?"

"*Da.*"

"I was told by his men that you owe him something," he says with concern.

My eyes narrow. "I did not expect to live after my father's death but, because of Nikolay's interference, both my father and I are still alive."

I glance at him, the pain intensifying when I confess, "I watched her die, *moy droog*…but was helpless to prevent it. I need that bastard to die but I've failed in that, too."

"What about your brothers? Why can't they help you? By God, there are four of them!"

I shut my eyes at the mention of my brothers. "That is the greatest cruelty of all. My brothers banned me from her funeral but let my father attend."

"That makes absolutely no sense!" he growls.

I open my eyes to meet his gaze. "My brothers are cowards like my father. We should all be put out of our misery and rid the world of the Durov taint."

"You are not allowed to talk like that."

I refuse to put up with Thane's demands any longer and dismiss him with a wave. "I don't want you here. Go home."

Thane pulls up his sleeve and shows me the scar on his wrist. "We are in this together, damn it. Remember, *brother*?"

I look down at the scar, frowning. "I didn't know how bad it would get when I made that vow with you." I place my hand on Thane's shoulder and say solemnly, "I'm sorry, but I want to die."

I can feel his palpable anger building. "No, damn it! You are not going to die. We vowed that we would be there for each other—and I will not fail you."

He gets to his feet, demanding I stand with him. "You are not the coward your father is. You will not only survive this, but you will also exact justice for your mother's murder. Someday, the pain of this moment will become the catalyst for you to do great things. I know that both your mother and Tatianna expect you to be strong, to endure, and to live a life that would make them proud."

His words tear at my heart.

I want to join them, but he's right. They both would expect me to endure.

"I'm tired and broken. I have nothing left."

"Which is why I'm here," he answers firmly.

I gaze deep into his eyes and plead, "Just let me go."

"Never."

My heart hurts for him when I explain, "You don't understand, *moy droog*. You are doomed if you stay with me."

"I don't care."

And he doesn't. Thane would die for me and knowing that breaks me. My voice is gruff when I admit, "I could not handle losing you."

"We will survive this, I promise. But you can't give up or you condemn us both."

"That is not fair, comrade."

"What? You take a vow to live, then try to commit suicide at the hands of ruffians by picking fights with them? That, my friend, is not fair."

"I hate you, brother," I snarl, angry that he's so fucking stubborn.

"You're a selfish prick."

"Have I ever stated any differently?"

Thane chuckles, his eyes softening. "No, but I match your level of selfishness with my level of stubbornness. I'm like the never-ending waves hitting the rocks against the shore. I will wear you down to sand with my unyielding resolve."

"I already told you the Durov clan is not worth your time."

"Your family is not, but you, Anton Durov, are."

His words rile me up and I growl, "Did I express how much I thoroughly dislike you?"

"You've mentioned it a few times," he answers dryly.

I grit my teeth. "You're not only stubborn, but highly irritating."

"Like a wave against the rock."

I shake my head. "I'm already sick of your wave analogy."

Thane smirks. "Never-ending…"

I roar in frustration, punching the pillow next to me repeatedly, imagining it's Thane's face.

As angry as I am right now, I know the truth. In my darkest hour, I begged God for death, and He sent Thane to rescue me.

Brother

"Why did you come to Russia?" I finally ask Thane.

"When I still hadn't heard from you weeks after you left, I knew something was wrong." Thane frowns at me. "But I had no idea how bad it really was. Why didn't you reach out, brother?"

I glance away, muttering, "What was the point? You couldn't bring her back."

"I could have been here to support you."

I shake my head. "Thane, you only have one semester left. You've worked so hard. All those late nights and weekends should not be wasted…"

He shrugs. "It means nothing without you."

I swallow hard, realizing everything he is willing to sacrifice for me. "You still have enough time to catch up and finish your courses. I'm fine now."

Thane looks me in the eyes. "You may be able convince other people of that, but I'm not so easily fooled."

I snort. "What do you plan to do? Spend every day

babysitting me?"

"No, I'm not going to mother you. I will, however, push you every day until you are strong again."

I beat on my chest with my fist. "I'm plenty strong."

"Not here…" he says, resting his hand over my heart. "…not yet."

I chuckle harshly. "That will never heal, comrade."

"Someday it will."

He states it with such confidence that my heart starts to race.

"You would be a fool to give up on your education," I insist. "Don't you dare do that on my account."

"Actually, I'm doing this for me. The world would be a shitty place for me without you."

I look at him in disbelief. "Why is it you're so determined to keep me around when my brothers are so quick to throw me out?"

"Simple. They are fools, and I am not. Don't waste energy concerning yourself with fools."

I sigh as I stare down at the scar on my wrist. "I'm unsure if you are a blessing or a curse, Thane Davis."

He smiles. "I'm a little of both."

Thane is not exactly the nurturing type. In fact, he's relentless—not allowing me a moment's peace. He doesn't coddle. No, he makes me work hard every day, pushing me when my heart isn't in it, and demanding my best.

I feel sorry for whoever ends up being his collared sub, I think ruefully.

One morning, I wake up from a nightmare and am so overwhelmed with grief that I struggle even to get out of bed.

Rather than chastise me, Thane asks, "What do you need right now?"

I have to bite my tongue and not say the first thing that comes to my mind.

I want my mother alive.

Knowing that is not my reality, I tell him, "I'd like to collect a few things from my mother's."

"Absolutely."

I'm glad to have him with me. I haven't been to the manor since the day she died, and my nerves are still painfully raw. When we walk up to the door, I hesitate for a moment as I go to unlock it.

"I'm right here," Thane reassures me.

I nod, slip the key into the lock, and turn it. Holding my breath, I walk into the place.

It is eerily quiet, amplifying the sound of our footsteps as we walk down the hallway.

"How can I help?" he asks.

"I want every photo album you find."

"Okay. I'll start here," he states, heading into the room on the right.

I search other rooms on the lower level, but purposely avoid the kitchen. I'm not sure I'm ready to face the kitchen without my mother in it.

Thane eventually returns with several albums and hands them to me. "I was thorough. This is everything I could find."

There are not nearly enough here between us. My mother shared so many more albums with me that last day together, and I realize the rest must be upstairs. I groan inside.

I had hoped to avoid the upstairs, but now I must steel myself for it.

"There are more."

Thane senses my hesitancy and offers, "I can get them for you. No reason to put yourself through that."

I shake my head, understanding it is something I must do. I was not there for her funeral and did not get the chance to look upon her face one last time. No, my family stole that from me.

I need closure, so I slowly walk up the stairs, but each step is more difficult than the last. When I make it to the landing, I turn to face the room where she died. Instead of circumventing it, I head straight toward it.

I don't know what I will see when I open the door and my heart pounds heavily as I turn the knob and the door swings open.

Whatever I was expecting…it isn't this.

The carpet has been replaced, and every single item in the room has been carefully returned to its original position.

It looks…normal.

My heart aches. I wasn't prepared for this. I feel the room should have been cordoned off, a reminder of the tragedy that took place here. Instead, it's as if the violence of her death has been erased.

"Is this where it happened?" Thane asks quietly as I

stare at the area beside the window.

I nod.

Standing there, staring down at the spot where she died, I realize her spirit isn't here.

I look around and notice several photo albums in the bookshelves. "Let's grab those and leave."

"You don't need time alone here?"

"*Nyet.*"

I head to my mother's bedroom next and am devastated to find her room has been cleared of all her personal belongings.

"What is this?" I cry, checking the closet and every drawer. "They've taken everything that belonged to her."

Thane shakes his head, looking as disturbed as I feel.

"How can family be so cruel?" I growl. "I was banned from the funeral, and now I'm robbed of her things as well?"

I walk from her bedroom to the room where I was staying and find all my things have disappeared as well. I close my eyes.

I have been disowned.

I have no family now.

Except…

I turn to Thane. "I appreciate you more than you know, brother."

"The feeling is mutual."

I push back the pain, refocusing my efforts to make sure I have every album in the house before we head back downstairs.

Looking at the kitchen, I feel drawn to it now.

I place the large stack of albums I'm carrying on the

hallway table and walk into the kitchen as memories of our last meal together flood my mind.

I glance around my mother's kitchen, recalling the delicious aroma of her cooking while the sound of her joyous laughter rings in my head. Opening the kitchen drawer, I pull out her rolling pin and clutch it to my chest. *"Mamulya…"*

I see a vision of her smiling face and leave the room lighter of heart.

Balancing the rolling pin on top of the stack, I pick up the photo albums, securing the rolling pin under my chin as Thane and I make our way out to the vehicle.

"Is that really all you want from here?" Thane asks before shutting the trunk.

"Da." I look back at the manor, knowing it is the last time I will ever come here.

Suddenly feeling nostalgic, I decide there is someone I want Thane to meet. "Do you mind if we take a detour on the way back?"

"Not at all."

I drive over to Titov's place, telling Thane, "This is the guy I've talked about. Tatianna's brother."

Thane looks at me warily. "You aren't planning to hurt him?"

I chuckle, understanding his fear. "We have reconciled. It was my mother's last wish."

Thane looks at me solemnly. "That must not have been easy for you."

I shake my head. It's true, but not for the reason he thinks.

After we pull up to Titov's, I knock on the door,

hoping he's home. To my relief, he opens the door but stares distrustfully at Thane.

"Who is this?"

"This is my American brother, Thane Davis."

Titov nods curtly but seems unhappy to see him.

"Rytsar has often spoken of you," Thane offers, putting his hand out.

Titov glances at me warily before shaking his hand. "I'm sure Rytsar had nothing good to say, then."

Clearing his throat, Thane answers truthfully, "Nothing good until today."

Titov looks at me strangely. "What is this about, Rytsar?"

I put one arm around Titov's shoulder and the other around Thane's. "It would have pleased *Mamulya* to see the three of us together, Titov."

Tears immediately come to his eyes and he nods.

Titov steps aside and tells Thane, "Join me for a drink in honor of her."

I punch Titov in the shoulder to show him my gratitude as I walk past and enter his place.

We sit at the small kitchen table while Titov gets three shot glasses and a bottle. When he sets them on the table, he announces, "I'm out of pickles."

I shake my head, *tsking.* "That is a major failure on your part."

He throws up his hands. "You didn't tell me you were coming."

"Which is a failure on Durov's part," Thane states, looking at me.

Titov stares at Thane as if in shock. He has never

heard anyone speak to me like that before. He suddenly breaks out in a grin, declaring, "I can already tell I'm going to like you, Thane Davis."

"Pour the vodka, Titov," I bark, sensing these two together might prove troublesome for me.

As he pours, Titov asks me, "What have you been up to? I expected you to come by sooner after our discussion."

I know he is anxious to avenge Tatianna, and I don't want to explain what my state of mind has been over the last few weeks, so I divert the conversation. "Thane and I went to collect *Mamulya's* things today, but my father has cleared the house of her."

Titov looks as crushed as I feel. "That man must die!" he states emphatically, then glances quickly at Thane.

I shake my head once to let Titov know that Thane is ignorant of our plan to end Vladimir Durov's life.

He takes my cue and immediately lifts his glass. "To your mother. An exceptional woman and one of the kindest souls I've ever met."

Thane and I lift our glasses and then down the shots in unison.

Titov pours another round and I attempt to make my toast but choke up as I speak. "*Mamulya* is…smiling down on us right now."

"Agreed," Titov says solemnly, throwing back his shot.

When Titov fills the glasses again, I tell Thane, "Do not feel you must toast her, comrade."

He frowns. "But I want to." Holding up his glass,

Thane looks at me.

"Your passion for life, your loyalty to others, and that keen wit are reflective of your mother. Although I've never met her, I feel as if I know her because of who you are. As long as you are alive, she will continue to influence the world."

"Well said," Titov exclaims, slamming the shot glass down on the table after he drinks it.

I stare at Thane, moved by his words. I have to swallow the growing lump in my throat before I can down my own shot. He is truly my brother in every way that matters.

I spend the afternoon listening to Titov share the adventures of our youth while Thane offers Titov a look into our lives in LA. Both men are fascinated by each other's stories about me.

I get the privilege of sitting back and simply listening to them.

Titov represents my life before Tatianna's death and Thane represents my life after. Hearing them talk, I start to get a better sense of who I was, who I am now, and who I am meant to be.

For the first time since my mother's death, I feel a glimmer of hope for my future.

I look up toward the heavens and smile.

I will make you both proud.

Retribution

It takes two whole months of brotherly love and numerous kicks in the ass before Thane feels comfortable enough to return home to America. As much as I hate to see him go, I feel good about his departure.

He and I both have things to accomplish before we can move forward with our lives. He needs to graduate, and I need to take care of my father.

Walking toward his departure gate, Thane asks one more time, "You'll call if you need me?"

I slap him on the back. "If you ask me that again, I will punch you in the face."

"But you'll call?"

I'm reminded of his analogy about acting like a wave in the ocean and I burst out laughing. "Yes, *moy droog*, I will call you."

When the overhead speaker announces his flight is boarding, Thane stands up. "Well, I'm headed out."

"I will miss you, brother," I say, pulling him into a hug. "Thank you."

"Always, brother." Thane slaps me on the back several times before letting go. He turns to leave, handing his ticket to the stewardess.

I feel a sense of profound camaraderie as I watch his plane take off.

I owe that man my life—literally.

My loyalty to him will never waver.

After my father heads out for the night with a new piece of arm candy, I return to the family estate.

I seek out Nadia, our cook, and ask to speak with her privately.

She has worked for our family for almost forty-five years, starting out as a housemaid at the age of sixteen. She is a robust woman of sixty who doesn't take shit from anyone, but she has a heart of gold and a soft spot for me.

"Nadia, I want to ask something from you that is extremely risky, but the reward will be equally as great."

"I'm not interested in money schemes," she states respectfully. "I won't do it for your father, and I won't do it for you."

I look at her in surprise, disgusted that my father has asked such a thing of her. "I would never involve you in something so crass," I assure Nadia. "What I'm proposing would result in justice for my mother."

Her eyes suddenly light up. "How I can help?"

I appreciate her willingness, but warn Nadia again,

"What I need would require your utmost care, trust, and complete silence. No one can know what happens or both of our lives will be forfeit."

She waves off my concern. "I've lived enough years not to fear death."

I love this woman.

"Everything I tell you must go with you to your grave."

"I would never betray your confidence," she states matter-of-factly.

Damn, I love her even more.

I look at Nadia solemnly when I tell her, "My father sent the assassin who killed my mother."

She frowns but does not look surprised. Why would she? She knows what a vile man he is because she has served our family her entire life. I thank God she is not a fool like my brothers.

"I plan to kill him, Nadia. However, I need your help to do it."

She doesn't even blink an eye. "Go on."

"It must to be done in such a way that no one will question his death, so I plan to use poison."

She nods, now understanding her role in this. "What kind of poison?"

"Ricin."

"Yes, that will do."

Although I'm surprised she's familiar with the substance, I am also grateful for it. "There is no antidote, so even if I'm caught, he will die regardless."

"*Da*," she answers simply, not at all rattled by the nature of our conversation.

"I will be the one to deliver the lethal dose."

She frowns. "What will I be doing, then?"

"We must first establish that he is ill. I need you to add this to his food." I hand her a vial. "The powder is made from Madanaphala fruit and will induce vomiting. Slowly increase the dosage until everyone is convinced he's becoming seriously sick. Once that has been established, I will arrange for my father to be transferred to a private hospital where I can treat him myself.

I see a hint of a smile on her face.

"If you need time to think this over, please do."

"All these years, I have endured your terrible cries during those beatings and your mother's silent tears because of that man. It will not be a problem for me."

If Nadia were the hugging type, I would hug her right now. Instead, I shake her hand firmly. "Of course, I will see to it that you are compensated."

"The only compensation I need is to see Vladimir in the ground."

Placing my hand on my chest, I tell her sincerely, "You are a woman after my own heart."

She looks at me with an almost tender expression on her normally stoic face. "I was there the day you were born, and I spent every day with you in this house." Her face suddenly turns beet red. "I don't know if it is appropriate to say this, but the truth is you are like a son to me."

Her statement slams me in the chest and leaves me speechless.

Once again, I'm reminded that family comes from the heart and not by blood.

Weeks later, Nadia's carefully administered care pays off and I receive news that Vladimir is extremely ill. When his regular doctor fails to relieve his symptoms, I anonymously send a specialist who informs my father that he's familiar with the condition and asks to examine him.

Out of desperation, my father agrees.

After his examination, the "doctor" concludes that my father would be better served at his private hospital. Vladimir refuses, certain it is a simple stomach flu, and sends him away.

However, it only takes a week before my father sends for the specialist again because he can't keep anything down and his ass is sore from constant diarrhea.

He makes arrangements to be transferred to the private hospital, and my four brothers take him there personally, wanting to evaluate the place themselves. They leave the facilities satisfied he is under excellent care.

I have the staff continue his daily dosage with a new diet of porridge, which is now delivered by a comely nurse. Despite being violently ill, the pathetic bastard flirts with her as he consumes his own sickness.

On the day of reckoning, I call Titov and tell him to meet me there.

I have waited for this day ever since I watched my mother die in my arms and learned of his treachery in connection with Tatianna's kidnapping.

"Are you ready for this?" I ask Titov, wondering if

he may be having second thoughts about killing a man.

His eyes flash with anger. "I was ready the day Tatianna was taken from us."

I nod in agreement.

We walk into the room together.

"Father," I say in a low, icy tone.

His eyes dart up and I revel in the look of terror on his face.

"That's right, Father. I've come to collect on my debt, and I brought a friend with me." Turning to Titov, I say, "You remember Tatianna's brother, don't you?"

His eyes widen with fear and he starts pressing the nurse's button repeatedly, crying out for help.

The pretty nurse comes in and smiles at him before walking over to me. I kiss her on the lips. "You have done well," I praise her, grabbing the back of her neck in order to kiss her more deeply.

When I let go, I smack her on the ass. "You may go now."

She bows and then looks over at my father and gives him a cute little wave goodbye.

Vladimir's jaw hangs open, realizing there is no one to rescue him from his fate.

"Grab a seat and let's sit for a chat," I tell Titov.

We drag chairs to opposite sides of the bed and sit down.

"This isn't right," Vladimir tells me in his stern, fatherly voice.

I laugh, remembering when that tone used to bring fear to my young heart. "What isn't right, Father? The fact that you killed Tatianna, or the fact that you had

Mamulya's throat slit?"

"I have no idea what you're talking about."

"I know about the inheritance."

His eyes flash with fear. "Whoever told you that is playing you for a fool, Anton."

"Really? Is that why Nikolay has given me permission to kill you?"

"Liar! The Koslovs would never allow such a thing. I'm under their protection."

"Unfortunately, the Koslov brothers are not in charge. It was stupid of you to think they were." I move in closer. "Whatever deal you made with them is null and void."

His eyes grow wide and he shakes his head. "All lies!"

"Two innocent women are dead because of you."

He clamps his mouth shut, refusing to speak.

I graze the back of my hand against his cheek before I slap it hard.

The feared sadist, Vladimir Durov, lets out a whimpering cry.

"I always knew you were a coward," I tell him.

He steels his jaw and glares at me. "You will be dead if you go through with this."

I smile grimly. "We're all going to die, Father. However, most of us don't know the hour of our death." I look up at the clock. "You have exactly one."

I watch his heart race on the monitor as he stares at the clock.

"Why don't we talk man to man? I might let you live."

He glares at me distrustfully.

"Go ahead, Titov. Ask him anything."

Titov's eyes are full of murderous anger. "Tatianna was an innocent, you motherfucking bastard!"

Vladimir shrugs, seemingly immune to Titov's pain. "So? The cunt wanted to fuck Anton. That was enough reason to sell her."

Before I can stop him, Titov has his hands wrapped around Vladimir's throat.

I pry him away and look Titov in the eye. "No marks."

Titov snarls, but nods, shooting daggers of hate toward my father. "You knew nothing about her, but you sold her to a slaver and condemned her to death!"

"Her only responsibility was to pleasure men. If she couldn't handle that, she must have been weak. I've done much worse to my own subs and none of them died from it."

Both Titov and I cannot contain our fury and risk ending him prematurely. Fortunately, I've come prepared and hold up a thin hand towel and spray bottle of water, handing them to Titov. "Waterboarding will have the same effect as strangulation but will leave no marks. Have at it."

I look at the clock before I leave the room, telling Vladimir, "It looks like you only have fifty minutes left." I see the heart rate monitor spike, and I smile to myself as I leave Titov to reconcile Tatianna's death by spending time alone with the man.

I don't return for a full thirty minutes, but when I head back into the room, I find Vladimir's arms now tied to the rails of the bed. He is silent. His pupils are wide with fear as his eyes remained glued on Titov.

Titov nods to me before leaving the room.

I walk over to my father and glare at him, letting the minutes slowly tick down.

"I loved Tatianna like you loved *Mamulya.*"

"I know," he croaks. "That's why she was chosen."

My heart starts racing as I clench my fists, furious that I can't end him with my own hands. Through gritted teeth, I ask, "If you loved her, why did you kill *Mamulya?*"

"It's your fault my wife is dead!" he cries out. I'm shocked to see tears in his eyes. He looks up at me, unleashing his wrath. "I did everything in my power to get rid of you, but like the cockroach you are, you wouldn't die. That beautiful woman is dead because of you."

I stare at him, completely numb.

"If you had killed yourself, she would still be alive today. I blame you for losing her."

I narrow my eyes. "How can money mean that much to you?"

"You know nothing about life. Without money, you're nothing."

"Before you die…" I look up at the clock. "…in approximately twelve minutes, I want you to know that you will be erased from history. I will see to it personally. No one will know your name, and no one will ever speak of you again. As far as history and the rest of the world are concerned, you never existed."

I see the terror in his eyes, and he screams at me, "I

wish you had never been born!"

I look up at the clock again, "In eight minutes, it will be as if you never were."

He shakes his head. "Don't do this. I'm certain we can work something out, son."

I resent him calling me that, and growl, "I am not your son!"

He smiles. "Like it or not, you are."

I snort, looking at the clock. "Not in six more minutes."

The monitor spikes again and he stammers, "You… you will go to hell if you do this."

"So?"

"God will never let you reunite with either of them if you murder me."

"I will gladly suffer hell knowing their killer was brought to justice. Tatianna is dead, my mother is dead, and now you will be, too."

My father suddenly blurts out, "I've had a man trailing you."

"Your man isn't very good," I laugh, remembering the out of shape stalker I chased in the dark.

"You were supposed to return home when I left the threat with your friend. But you couldn't even do that right."

I raise an eyebrow. "So that was you?"

He nods, giving me a superior look. "When you failed to return to Russia, I put out a contract on your friends. That gorgeous blonde will be the first casualty."

I actually laugh and look up at the clock again. "You only have four minutes left."

"The only way to prevent their deaths is to release me now."

"Actually, Father, it will be easy enough to track him down now that I know you were the one who hired him. My friends will be fine."

I get up and walk to the door, letting Titov back in. I pick up the rubber gloves and slip them on, looking at Vladimir.

Picking up a small black vial, I ask, "Do you know what's in here?"

He shakes his head, staring at the bottle.

"Ricin."

"There's no need to do this," he cries hysterically. "I'll leave the country and you'll never hear from me again."

"You're right. We won't," Titov tells him.

Vladimir shakes his head in terror, looking desperately at me. "Don't do this, son."

I take the syringe and fill it with the liquid inside the vial. "Would you like to do the honors?" I ask Titov.

In answer, he put gloves on and takes the syringe.

"Don't kill me!" Vladimir cries, whimpering like a child.

"Don't worry," Titov assures him. "You won't die unless you are weak."

We both watch the clock count down to the last second. Titov then inserts the needle into the IV and releases the ricin into his system.

The monitor explodes with alarms. I press the button to turn them off.

As the two of us head to the door, I turn back and

smile. "I failed to mention that death is not instantaneous. Enjoy the next thirty-six hours, Father."

I leave the room knowing Vladimir will never hurt another person.

I have a sense of immense relief and vindication as we drive away...

I head to the countryside with Titov, driving for hours until we end up at a ridge overlooking the small town of Plyos.

As the night sky lights up with stars, we lay on the hood of my car and stare up at them in silence.

"Now what?" Titov asks.

"I'm not sure," I answer, folding my arms behind my head as I look up at the shimmering sky.

"I have waited for this moment for years, and now I feel satisfied...but empty. There has to be something more," he laments.

I think back on the conversation the three of us had when Thane and Titov were sharing stories about me, and the conviction I felt about my future.

"I know what it is," I tell him.

He turns his head toward me. "What?"

"We help others like Tatianna."

"How?"

"We keep our eyes open and act. We can't be blind to the suffering around us." I look at him, feeling heartbroken. "If just one person had acted, Tatianna would be alive right now."

Titov sighs deeply. "I will never forgive myself for what happened to her."

"This isn't on you. If anything, I'm the one to blame because of her association with me."

Titov stares at me. "I would never blame you. You loved Tatianna as much as I did."

"But I was unjustifiably cruel to you."

He shrugs. "You did everything in your power to save her. That's the only thing that matters to me."

"And you were with me every step of the way. All I have to hold onto is the fact that Tatianna was loved and cared for before she died."

"At least we have that," Titov says sadly, looking back up at the sky. "You mother explained to me how much you loved my sister. Knowing that helped me understand why you acted the way you did."

"She was my soulmate, Titov. I planned to marry her and treat her like a queen."

"Even though I didn't want to hear that as her big brother, it was obvious to me how she felt about you. She was hopelessly in love."

I shake my head, holding back the tears. "Life is cruel."

"It is."

"I've come to realize that everything we are rests on a fragile stack of expectations. When just a few are stripped away, we suddenly realize how truly vulnerable we are."

"True," he replies somberly.

We lay there in silence as an owl hoots in a far-off

tree.

"I think I will go back to America," I tell him. "I want to be there when my brother graduates."

I can hear the regret in his voice when he says, "There is nothing here for you anymore."

I prop myself up on my elbows and smile at him. "I would like you to come with me."

Titov looks both surprised and relieved. "Really?"

"I'm about to come into a lot of money and I need men I trust around me."

After the coroner performs a preliminary autopsy and pronounces Vladimir Durov dead of natural causes, I return to my father. By passing money across the right palms, I am given time alone with my father's body the day before the funeral.

When I walk into the room, I'm angered to see the peaceful expression on his face. My father doesn't deserve peace.

He was a violent man who unleashed his violence on me repeatedly as a little boy.

I did not get the satisfaction of killing him with my bare hands and the rage I still carry will not be denied.

I become that young boy again, but this time I return his violence with violence, enjoying the pain as my fist meets bone.

I will never be anyone's whipping boy again!

Afterward, I leave the room, feeling empowered. I

inform the staff that it will be a closed casket service and order them to seal it.

The day of his funeral, I leave for America with Titov. I've already identified the man my father contracted and have had him dealt with.

With the past now closed, I can concentrate my energy on the future ahead.

Rebirth

"What do you mean there will be no graduation ceremony?" I complain loudly in the middle of the outdoor commons.

Thane chuckles. "They don't have them mid-year."

"But you've put all that effort into getting that diploma early." I look to Anderson for validation. "Don't you agree he deserves a ceremony?"

The cattleman grins. "I do."

I look at Thane again. "And I came all the way from Russia to celebrate with you." I spit on the ground. "This college sucks!"

Students passing by laugh under their breaths.

"There is only one thing to be done," I growl in disgust.

"Don't feel obligated to do anything," Thane tells me. "I don't need fanfare. I just need the diploma coming in the mail."

I tsk. "What? They can't even be bothered to hand it to you personally?"

Thane smirks. "Such is the life of a mid-year graduate."

Anderson sweeps his hair back. "I'd gladly give up all the hoopla to be graduating with Thane now." Shaking his head, he frowns slightly. "It was hell without you guys here, and now I'm facing another semester just like it."

I look at Anderson and realize how much he has changed since the last time I saw him. The cattleman has a toughness to him I haven't seen before. "What's been happening with you?"

He shrugs. "Not much. Just followed Thane's example and started applying myself more."

Thane claps Anderson on the back. "He has gone above and beyond me. The guy is going to graduate with a double major in Finance and Economics."

I look at Anderson in surprise. "Why?"

"I figure if I'm going to dedicate myself to something, I may as well give it a hundred percent."

I glance over at Thane. "Did aliens replace our fun-loving cattleman while I was gone?"

Anderson smiles charmingly. "Without you disrupting my daily life, I've found I have a lot of extra time on my hands."

Anderson's admiration of Thane has always been obvious to me, but it's even more apparent now. He's taken a more focused attitude, but I wonder if he's lost a part of himself in the process.

It seems inevitable that each of us has redefined himself by weathering the unexpected curves life has thrown our way. Looking at the three of us, I realize how much we've changed.

Thane came in with blinders on, wanting to suffer through college for as short a time as possible. I came here wanting to escape my past, and Anderson just wanted to party.

We are not those boys anymore.

Thane is dedicated to helping those around him, I'm no longer running, and Anderson has become the college MVP. I chuckle to myself. Who would have thought it?

But this never would have happened if the three of us hadn't met that freshman year. It took all three of us knowing each other to shape us into the men standing here today.

Anderson takes me aside for a moment. "My entire family is deeply sorry to hear about your mother."

I nod, unable to respond without breaking down.

"My parents want me to tell you that you are welcome to visit anytime. And my mama says that when you are ready, she would love to learn some of your mother's favorite recipes."

I can't help tearing up. I am truly touched by his mother's thoughtfulness.

Anderson slaps me on the back, immediately apologizing. "I'm sorry, man. Didn't mean to upset you."

I shake my head. "Don't be sorry, cattleman. I appreciate it." But I walk away to regain my composure.

Naturally, Thane comes up to check on me. "Everything okay?"

I glance in Anderson's direction. "Absolutely, *moy droog*. It's good to be back."

Not someone to ignore the elephant in the room, I

ask, "How is Samantha?"

Thane takes a deep breath, obviously caught off guard that I'm going there so soon. However, he takes it in stride and answers, "She is doing well, considering."

"Explain."

"She's currently under the ownership of Blaze, the Mistress at the private party downtown."

"Ah…the fire specialist."

"Yes, and from what I've heard, Samantha is doing well serving under her. But, to help her grow, Blaze has been inviting different Doms to work with her, so she'll have a wide range of experiences and techniques to move forward with."

"Good."

"And, as far as AA, she hasn't touched a drop since that night and is doing well on her twelve-step program. She even visited both Anderson and me asking for forgiveness."

I raise my eyebrows. "Did you forgive her, comrade?"

He meets my gaze. "Yes, but only for those transgressions against me."

"As it should be." I nod, satisfied with his answer.

We stand there in silence for a moment before I ask, "Do you still fear for her mental state?"

He sighs heavily. "I won't lie. Samantha continues to struggle with the guilt of what she's done, but she has been faithfully attending her counseling sessions and I'm no longer afraid she'll harm herself."

Putting my hand on his shoulder, I tell him. "Continue your vigilance, comrade."

"I will never stop."

I nod again, knowing Thane is a man of his word. "So, what are your plans now that college is behind you?"

Thane's eyes instantly light up. "I already have a job lined up. I'll be working for a company based in LA that needs an organizational and efficiency trainer. I actually start next week."

I'm truly impressed by my comrade's tenacity. "So, the next phase of your life begins."

"I have it all planned out. First, I'll repay my uncle for his financial help in getting me through college, then I'll start saving for my own business."

"You don't plan to stay with this company?"

"Not for long. This will be the first step of many. My ultimate goal is to run my own company consulting with businesses around the world."

"Not a man of small dreams, are you?" I joke.

"What's that?" Anderson asks, walking up to us.

"I take it you already know what our friend has planned for the future?" I ask him.

Anderson grins. "Thane isn't one to sit on the sidelines."

I turn back to my comrade. "I always knew you would end up training people, but I thought it would lean in the direction of serving the BDSM community."

His lips twitch.

I raise an eyebrow. "What is it you aren't telling me?"

"We heard about your little discussion with Mr. Gallant," Anderson informs me.

"And…?" I prod.

Thane rubs his chin thoughtfully. "I've been invited to take their Dominant Training course under the direction of Master Nosh."

It makes perfect sense that the staff at the Training Center has asked him to take the course because it will give them a better idea of what Thane is capable of. "I have no doubt you will graduate at the top of your class, *moy droog*."

"To be honest, I'm more excited about the training course than about starting my own career." He hits me in the arm. "Thanks for messing with my focused plans."

I smirk proudly. "Anytime, brother."

For Thane's graduation, I go all out to make up for the college's lack of decorum. With the help of our mutual friends, as well as my family friend, Pyotr Gagarin, it becomes a truly momentous affair.

I have Anderson agree to blindfold Thane and drive him to the destination. When Thane steps out of Anderson's vehicle, it's clear he's not happy—which I find amusing.

"Why the sour face, *moy droog*?"

"I told you not to do anything, and now you have me being led around like a blind fool? Can I take this damn blindfold off now?"

"You may not," Anderson answers for me. "A lot of time and effort has gone into this graduation ceremony, buddy. You're not allowed to ruin it for us."

"You? I thought this was supposed to be for me."

I put my arm around Thane. "*Moy droog*, it was never about you."

"I figured as much…"

We lead him through the large home and down the curved staircase to the veranda below.

"Where are we?" he asks as we walk.

I say nothing, smiling to myself. Thane has no idea what's in store for him.

Anderson and I escort him to the center of the veranda and stand on either side of him. "On the count of three, you can take your blindfold off."

Everyone gathered counts down with me. "One…two…three!"

Thane rips his blindfold off and his jaw drops as he takes in the awesomeness.

Yes, I have totally outdone myself.

Pyotr Gagarin's impressive home overlooks the LA skyline, and the view from the veranda is truly inspiring. But what seems to have Thane in shock are the number of people who've come to celebrate his achievement.

I have invited every person I know who has influenced Thane during his college career, from his dungeon mates and lab partners, to his aunt and uncle.

"What have you done?" he mutters when he spots his two relatives mingling with the others.

"It was nothing," I answer proudly.

"You've brought them all together in one place? Are you mad?"

"*Da*," I answer proudly. I don't see the harm in it as I have let everyone know to dress formally for the event.

No one is walking around in leather or latex.

"What if they talk to each other?"

"That's what people normally do, comrade."

Thane turns to Anderson next. "And you let him do this?"

"Looking at the expression on your face right now was reason enough, buddy." He points to our dungeon friends. "Don't they clean up nice?"

Pointing to a handful of subs, I lean in to tell Thane, "After the party, the girls have something special planned for you."

The girls wave enthusiastically at Thane as his aunt and uncle come up to greet him.

The blush I see creeping over my comrade's cheeks is totally worth the twelve-hour plane trip from Russia.

"I'm impressed by how many people speak so highly of you," his uncle states. "It makes me prouder than I can say."

"Thanks, Unc. I consider myself lucky to know everyone here."

"And the girls are adorable," my aunt gushes. "They just love the brownies I brought."

Thane smiles kindly. "I bet they do, Auntie. Everyone loves your brownies."

He looks at his uncle again, probing him with a question, "Interesting mix of people, wouldn't you say?"

"You've really come into your own. I never imagined you'd have so many friends when you started college."

"And *girlfriends*," his aunt adds, giggling at him.

The subs wave at him again and, when his aunt waves back, it causes Thane to blush again. Little does she know what Thane's "girlfriends" have planned for him later tonight.

"It's interesting—the various ages of everyone and the fact that many of them don't go to your college. How did you end up meeting them, anyway?" his uncle asks.

Thane turns to me. "Durov brought us together, and I have to say I'm extremely grateful he did."

Anderson wraps an arm around my shoulders, grinning. "That makes two of us."

"You are a very interesting man, Mr. Durov, based on everything I've heard," his uncle states. "I'd like to hear more about how you and Thane met."

Thane mutters. "I'll tell you all about it sometime later, Unc."

I'm curious about how much he *will* be telling his uncle and smile to myself. Slapping Thane on the back, I say, "I know I'm fascinating, but today we are here to honor you, comrade."

His uncle turns toward Thane with a look of sincere admiration. "We are extremely proud of you, Thane. You've remained determined despite everything you've been through."

His aunt grabs Thane's arm and squeezes it. "Of course, we're proud! You graduated early and already have a job. How could we not be proud?"

If Thane were a crying man, I think he would be shedding a tear or two. Even though these two people are not his parents, the love they have for him is undeniable.

Thane smiles stiffly, reining in his emotions. He turns to challenge me. "Got anything else?"

"As a matter of fact, I do, *moy droog.*"

I whistle, and everyone quickly takes their places as Professor Brooks walks out, dressed in her official college regalia.

Thane looks surprised when he sees her and gives me a questioning look.

I know how highly he regards the professor after taking her class his first year at college. What he may not be aware of is that she feels the same way toward him.

In the center of the veranda, Professor Brooks stands with her hands behind her back, smiling at the crowd. "I knew from the first moment I met Mr. Davis in my Photography 101 class that he was uniquely talented."

There are chuckles from several of the Doms in the crowd.

"As a photographer, he has an eye for the profound, and a deep sense of loyalty to those he photographs. Mr. Davis left quite an impression on me." She glances at Thane and nods. "It was truly a pleasure to have you in my class."

Looking back at everyone, she announces in a formal tone, "It is my honor and privilege to present Thane Lorenzo Davis with his diploma today."

She turns to him, revealing that she's holding the diploma in her hand.

When Thane doesn't move, Anderson and I give him a nudge forward.

I grin, feeling like a proud parent, as I watch Thane walk up to receive his diploma from the professor. She shakes his hand formally as she congratulates him.

The entire group breaks out in applause as Anderson and I whistle enthusiastically from the sidelines.

My heart swells with pride as Thane's friends crowd around him, wanting to add their own congratulations.

"You did good, doing all this for him," Anderson compliments.

I shrug. "It's the least I could do for the brother who saved my life."

To everyone, I shout, "Let the celebration begin. The vodka bar is now officially open!"

Hours later, Thane walks up beside me as I stare at the downtown skyline.

"I guess this marks the end of college for me," he states, sounding almost as if he's experiencing regret.

I turn my head and smile at him. "And a new beginning."

He nods, gazing thoughtfully at the tall skyscrapers in the distance.

Taking advantage of the seriousness of this moment, I say, "I wonder how many kids you will have."

Thane shakes his head, chuckling. "I can guarantee you that I'm never having kids. I plan on being a highly successful businessman, nothing more."

"Says the man who will have five of them."

"Don't even go there, Durov," he warns, elbowing me in the ribs.

We both laugh for a moment before he asks in a serious tone, "What do you plan to do now?"

I sigh in satisfaction as I watch the sun set over the city. "I'm about to make Tatianna and *Mamulya* proud…"

I hope you enjoyed *The Russian Reborn!*
COMING UP NEXT—*Tied to Hope: Brie's Submission,* Book 18 of the Brie Series
Yes, you heard me right!
A new book in the Brie's Submission Series
(Release Date – October 15, 2019)

Are you NEW to Brie and dying to find out what happens to Rytsar, Sir and Master Anderson?
Start reading the 1st box set of Brie's Submission.

COMING NEXT

Tied to Hope:
Brie's Submission

Available for Preorder

Reviews mean the world to me!
I truly appreciate you taking the time to review **The Russian Reborn**.
If you could leave a review on both Goodreads and the site where you purchased this eBook from, I would be so grateful. Sincerely, ~Red

You can continue the journey of Sir, Rytsar and Master Anderson with the 1st Box Set of *Brie's Submission* which is FREE!

Start reading NOW!

ABOUT THE AUTHOR

Over Two Million readers have enjoyed Red's stories

Red Phoenix – USA Today Bestselling Author
Winner of 8 Readers' Choice Awards

Hey Everyone!

I'm Red Phoenix, an author who also happens to be a submissive in real life. I wrote the Brie's Submission series because I wanted people everywhere to know just how much fun BDSM can be.

There is a huge cast of characters who are part of Brie's journey. The further you read into the story the more you learn about each one. I hope you grow to love Brie and the gang as much as I do.

They've become like family.

When I'm not writing, you can find me online with readers.

I heart my fans! ~Red

To find out more visit my Website

redphoenixauthor.com

Follow Me on BookBub

bookbub.com/authors/red-phoenix

Newsletter: Sign up

redphoenixauthor.com/newsletter-signup

Facebook: AuthorRedPhoenix

Twitter: @redphoenix69

Instagram: RedPhoenixAuthor

I invite you to join my reader Group!

facebook.com/groups/539875076052037

SIGN UP FOR MY NEWSLETTER
HERE FOR THE LATEST RED
PHOENIX UPDATES

SALES, GIVEAWAYS, NEW
RELEASES, EXCLUSIVE SNEAK
PEEKS, AND MORE!
SIGN UP HERE
REDPHOENIXAUTHOR.COM/NEWSLETTER-
SIGNUP

Red Phoenix is the author of:

Brie's Submission Series:
Teach Me #1
Love Me #2
Catch Me #3
Try Me #4
Protect Me #5
Hold Me #6
Surprise Me #7
Trust Me #8
Claim Me #9
Enchant Me #10
A Cowboy's Heart #11
Breathe with Me #12
Her Russian Knight #13
Under His Protection #14
Her Russian Returns #15
In Sir's Arms #16
Bound by Love #17
Tied to Hope #18

***You can also purchase the** AUDIO BOOK **Versions**

Also part of the Submissive Training Center world:

Captain's Duet
Safe Haven #1
Destined to Dominate #2

Rise of the Dominates Trilogy
Sir's Rise #1
Master's Fate #2
The Russian Reborn #3

Other Books by Red Phoenix

Blissfully Undone
* Available in eBook and paperback

(Snowy Fun—Two people find themselves snowbound in a cabin where hidden love can flourish, taking one couple on a sensual journey into ménage à trois)

His Scottish Pet: Dom of the Ages
* Available in eBook and paperback

Audio Book: *His Scottish Pet: Dom of the Ages*

(Scottish Dom—A sexy Dom escapes to Scotland in the late 1400s. He encounters a waif who has the potential to free him from his tragic curse)

The Erotic Love Story of Amy and Troy
* Available in eBook and paperback

(Sexual Adventures—True love reigns, but fate continually throws Troy and Amy into the arms of others)

eBooks

Varick: The Reckoning

(Savory Vampire—A dark, sexy vampire story. The hero navigates the dangerous world he has been thrust into with lusty passion and a pure heart)

Keeper of the Wolf Clan (Keeper of Wolves, #1)

(Sexual Secrets—A virginal werewolf must act as the clan's mysterious Keeper)

The Keeper Finds Her Mate (Keeper of Wolves, #2)

(Second Chances—A young she-wolf must choose between old ties or new beginnings)

The Keeper Unites the Alphas (Keeper of Wolves, #3)

(Serious Consequences—The young she-wolf is captured by the rival clan)

Boxed Set: Keeper of Wolves Series (Books 1-3)

(Surprising Secrets—A secret so shocking it will rock Layla's world. The young she-wolf is put in a position of being able to save her werewolf clan or becoming the reason for its destruction)

Socrates Inspires Cherry to Blossom

(Satisfying Surrender—A mature and curvaceous woman becomes fascinated by an online Dom who has much to teach her)

By the Light of the Scottish Moon

(Saving Love—Two lost souls, the Moon, a werewolf, and a death wish…)

In 9 Days

(Sweet Romance—A young girl falls in love with the new student, nicknamed "the Freak")

---

9 Days and Counting

(Sacrificial Love—The sequel to *In 9 Days* delves into the emotional reunion of two longtime lovers)

And Then He Saved Me

(Saving Tenderness—When a young girl tries to kill herself, a man of great character intervenes with a love that heals)

(Seeking Fulfillment—A desperate wife lives out her fantasies by taking five different men in five days)

Connect with Red on Substance B

Substance B is a platform for independent authors to directly connect with their readers. Please visit Red's Substance B page where you can:

- Sign up for Red's newsletter
- Send a message to Red
- See all platforms where Red's books are sold

Visit Substance B today to learn more about your favorite independent authors.